THE WRITER
&
THE GHOSTWRITER

Zoran Živković

FG-RS0020L2
ISBN: 978-4-908793-24-0

Cover: Youchan Ito, Togoru Art Works

Neoclassic Fleurons font used with permission of
Paulo W–Intellecta Design

Cadmus Press
cadmusmedia.org

THE WRITER

&

THE GHOSTWRITER

Zoran Živković

Translated from the Serbian
by
Alice Copple-Tošić

Cadmus Press
2018

Contents

The Writer

A very short novel, without chapters,
about writing and darkness

I SWITCHED ON THE computer.

First I pulled down the Venetian blind, of course. That was part of my morning ritual, and on sunny days like this one it had a practical function. Nevertheless, I also pull it down on cloudy days, superstitiously striving to maintain the ambience. My study looks to the east, and my desk faces a large window, so that, without the blind, I would have to squint and scowl until noon to see anything on the screen. This way there's no need to squint, but on cloudy days, for the sake of maintaining the ambience, I strain my eyes in unnecessary semidarkness.

Not that I pull it all the way down. I leave a gap of about fifteen centimeters above the windowsill, so that sunshine reaches the area where it is definitely welcome: an eight-sided glass vessel, set in the window. That vessel, formerly a small aquarium, has been converted to serve as a flowerpot for a group of miniature cactuses, the kind with very small pink and white flowers. Light also slants through the narrow slits between the horizontal plastic bars, creating shimmering arabesques in the dusky air of the room. Even if I sat with my back to the window, I think I would keep the blind down at such times of the day just to enjoy the transient play of bright and dark stripes on objects in the room. The peculiar impression of unreality thus created, one which (for reasons unknown to me) I find very stimulating, is enhanced by dust motes floating in the air, caught by diagonal beams of light. I know that some writers are not at all influenced by their immediate surroundings. For me, the ambient mood is almost everything.

The trouble, however, is that an appropriate ambience, while surely indispensable, is not sufficient for success in my work. If my environment alone mattered, I would have finished the book I am working on long ago. The environment being faultless, the book stalled nevertheless—and near the end, at that. When I began to write it, I had the impression, without clearly knowing why, that the thing would be a novel. However, matters took a different turn: episodes succeeded each other, but with so few connecting points that, as the writing progressed, there appeared before me something which would be (at best) a collection of loosely linked stories. Definitely not a novel.

I do not, of course, have anything against collections of stories, nor do I consider them intrinsically less valuable than novels, yet there started to creep over me a feeling, if not of disappointment, then definitely of expectations imperfectly fulfilled. Yet I did not despair of turning it around: what I had written could still grow from a conglomerate into an amalgam, but for this to happen, one more chapter was needed, the closing one, which would grab those only seemingly heterogeneous episodes and weave them into a whole. My intuition alone told me, and only in a whisper, that such a chapter was at all possible; but intuitions do not write, and that final chapter, required but by no means guaranteed, stubbornly refused to materialize.

I deliberately ascribe to that chapter the quality of volition, the ability to decide, quite independently of my wishes, whether it will or will not come into existence. I do this without any desire to undermine the proud authority over their own words to which certain other writers lay claim. Only in my own name do I speak, and solely on the basis of my personal experience of writing. In my case, the act of writing can hardly be called "creative"; I am, at best, perhaps an intermediary. . . .

When I sit at the keyboard, I experience only the vague tension of a go-between who expects to be used, certainly no sense of divine inspiration, least of all a godly trance in which I might see the entirety of the work in a single, all-encompassing vision, and then just sit down to perform the necessary technical chores, to type it up. Nothing like that with me; rather the opposite.

At the outset, I face a wall of darkness. I have no idea what I will write about, what will pop up on the screen. And then, especially if the environment is perfect, sentences begin to well up spontaneously from that darkness, while I watch with growing impatience to see how the thing will come out. If there is any recognizable stimulus prompting me to go on, it is this reader-like curiosity.

When I am reading some exciting or otherwise interesting work, written by one of my colleagues of the keyboard, the same curiosity drives me to fly through the pages; but when I write, there is an unfortunate physical limitation which prevents me from satisfying that curiosity anything like as fast as I want to. It is this: I type with only one finger—my right index finger—which, after decades of over-exploitation and maltreatment, has become markedly thicker and more gnarled than its fellows.

Although I manage quite a respectable speed for one finger, the swiftness with which it flies from key to key is far from sufficient to cope with my impatience. Yet when I tried to use the fruits of modern technology and replace the keyboard with a dictaphone, so that I might improve my speed enormously by just saying out loud those sentences which spontaneously arise from the darkness—then nothing at all emerged. The silence was total, as unrelieved as it was mysterious.

I spent several sessions of many minutes in front of that gadget; it was turned on, but its sensitive microphone failed to register anything except my tongue-tied impotence and those minute office noises which are normally disregarded or not heard at all: the hiss of curtains in a gentle flow of air, the creaking of the dry parquet, the progressively more fatigued buzzing of an insect who will pay with his life for his failure to comprehend the existence of a perfectly transparent yet impenetrable substance such as glass, the subdued sounds of the outside world going about its own business six floors below. . . .

A friend of mine, who unexpectedly dropped by for a visit yesterday, and to whom I confided my understandable frustrations with the act of writing, immediately explained to me, concisely and unambiguously as is his custom, what the problem was. That darkness, from which is born whatever I am writing (said he in the voice of authority), is nothing but my subconscious mind. It is, though, slightly odd, he remarked, wrinkling his forehead significantly and raising his eyebrows above the rim of his glasses, that subconsciousness will only express itself through one finger, instead of through the mouth, which would be far more natural and usual. So, in all probability, he concluded confidently, this has something to do with some repressed childhood experience, some unpleasantness which happened to me but which I am refusing consciously to confront.

As it happened we were in my study at the time, and I was sitting on a couch which, being covered with corduroy in a dark-purple floral pattern, has a strong calming effect; so he suggested that I should immediately stretch out on it while he remained in the nearby armchair. Then together we should try to "ferret out" (his expression) whatever obstacle was hindering me. First he asked me for a pencil and a notepad, and to unplug the telephone. This was a necessary condition, as the ringing of a phone unnerved him terribly at the best of times, even during an ordinary chat (which is why he had never had a phone installed in his apartment), and on an extraordinary occasion such as this it would be quite unconscionably distressing. Perhaps the only thing that rattled him more than a phone ringing was the barking of dogs.

At first I thought he was joking, but then, seeing that he meant it quite seriously, I had no option but to agree, although I did not feel at all inhibited by any gruesome experiences, and definitely none from childhood. Nor did I think that a man of letters like himself, and one without any experience as a parent (essential if one is to have any understanding whatsoever of children's difficulties, I think), would be the person best suited to undertake such "ferretings." I had only started to unburden myself to him in the first place because I was convinced that my problem was of a literary, not psychiatric, nature, although I grant that the distinction may not always be very clear-cut.

Thus did we come to spend the next hour and a half in an avid analytical search through the most bizarrely piquant details of my early childhood.

When did my mother stop breast-feeding me?

As if I could remember that! As far as my memory from that age goes, it may be that she never breast-fed me, that she had no milk and that I was on a bottle from day one. I do not know; we never talked about it, and it is far too late for me to ask her now.

Did my father often threaten me by shaking a finger at me and raising his voice, especially while I was on the potty?

Well, I only remember, foggily, that I shouted at the very top of my voice (whether on the potty or not, it was all the same) whenever I was truly determined to get something, and that it worked well as a method of browbeating my father, because he was, as I soon discovered, on the soft side.

Which finger did I prefer to suck?

I suspect that my friend had a concealed desire for me to say it was my unfortunate right index finger, but I had to disappoint him there: it was, as it is with all kids, my thumb. I did not tell him (because he did not ask, and also because I feared that it might sidetrack his investigation) that Mother once told me what a lot of trouble she had persuading me to stop sucking my thumb; in the end, when I was fully three years old, she had to smear quinine over it, so that I could not keep it in my mouth all the time.

Did I habitually wear items of female apparel?

Of course not! My mother's were too large and my sister's too small for me. But what's that got to do with anything?

There were many more questions, all in a similar tone, more or less shrewd or confusing, and I answered as truthfully and sincerely as seemed appropriate. My friend made diligent notes on the pad, taking very great care that, whenever I turned to him from the couch (mainly to glare at him suspiciously because of some question or other), I could not see what he was writing down. But, being a hopeless case of professorial absent-mindedness, when he ended his unusually lengthy visit he forgot to take the page with the notes along, although he surely meant to do so, because he remembered to tear it off the pad.

(This forgetfulness was by no means out of character. My home always contained at least one, and not infrequently all three, of the following items: his reading glasses, their thick old-fashioned frames fastened in one place with a piece of sticky tape already hard and brittle with age; his umbrella, from which a couple of bare ribs protruded; and his threadbare cap from which the cloth-covered central button had fallen off, no one remembers how long ago.)

This lucky circumstance gave me the opportunity

to satisfy my understandable, although—I confess—unconscionably indiscreet curiosity, and to peep into my own anamnesis. A surprise awaited me: there was no text at all, just a dense grid of thin, straight lines criss-crossing each other at various angles.

Try as I might, I was unable to decode that pattern; I turned it this way and that, held it so close to my eyes that the lines blurred, and so far away they blurred again, but to no avail. There was, of course, no question of asking my friend for an explanation, and I myself could conceive of only two: either he was using some very complex code, which would be superfluous, since his everyday handwriting was quite as indecipherable to everybody else as this gridwork puzzle, or he had been doing what people usually do when a pencil and paper are at hand but they have no real motive to do anything: he had just scrawled meaningless doodles, under the scholarly pretense of taking clinical notes.

Though frustrated over the anamnesis, I nevertheless obtained the diagnosis. Once he had finished his questions, my friend devoted a good ten minutes to considering his notes, voicing only an occasional "Hm!" or "Yeeeesss. . . ." The first sound gave the impression of deep thought, of serious concern, even, while the second was extended and seemed to end with both an exclamation point and a question mark. Both, of course, served to heighten my alarm as his quasi-patient, which was only partly relieved when I heard him pronounce final judgment on my case. That resolved certain matters only to bring forward new, unrelated problems—though by way of consolation, at least the new trouble had nothing to do with the traumas of my early life.

Essentially, I had no great reason to worry, my friend assured me at the end of the session; he spoke slowly, as one does when one hesitates and gropes for the words that will express one's meaning most precisely. The case was certainly interesting, primarily because it was unusual. Really, who would have expected the subconscious mind to find expression through a finger rather than a mouth? Most unusual. And extremely hard to fathom. But what mattered was that it was expressed. All I needed to do was to go on writing. I was free to do so, and it would be of some use. The subconscious mind would, eventually, regurgitate what it found too indigestible.

He never should have said that it would be "of some use." If he had refrained, matters would have ended harmlessly, then and there. He would have satisfied his weakness for grandiose posturing, which requires a grateful listener, and which was his main reason for visiting me; I am probably the last of the entire circle of his friends who still has the patience for such long and increasingly tedious exercises in intellectual exhibitionism. Although he always sits in the armchair and I on the couch during his visits, this had been the occasion for a reversal of our usual roles. Usually it is he who keeps talking, disgorging for my benefit the accumulated silt of a life filled, beneath a very thin veneer of success (professor at the University and, for one stop-gap term, even Head of Department), with various disappointments, rejections, frustrations, wrong choices and misanthropy.

I had been tolerant in letting myself be splashed with all that bile, that bitterness, that desperation, and at times I felt as I suppose all psychiatrists must feel: like a sponge with an unlimited capacity for soaking up dirty water, which makes the sponge heavier but doesn't alter its shape.

But I am not a professional psychiatrist, so at times deformations inevitably happen, when the sponge becomes too heavily saturated with dirt. Patience fails me mainly when his tone shifts from his usual ironic hauteur, which I can more or less endure, to the cynical or downright malicious, which always irritates me.

On such occasions, especially if they follow a bad day of my own, I stop acting the benevolent listener and start doing things I know will anger him. Harmless sponge turned into bristling sea urchin. Of course I know that such behavior is immature and that I will regret it later, but from time to time I am genuinely unable to resist the temptation. The livid rage which then comes over him gives me a satisfaction akin to the slaking of lust.

So I am supposed to keep writing mainly for therapeutic reasons, yes? Very flattering! Well, that could not go unpunished. I myself am allowed to hold my own writing in as low esteem as I like. I can berate it as insufficiently creative, etcetera—but what gave him the right to speak of it with such open contempt? On all previous occasions he had, at least, expressed himself obliquely, so that I had no excuse to claim insult and rebel.

I remember, the first time I told him of my attempts at prose composition, ingenuously expecting some support from him, he responded with a lengthy lecture that conveyed one basic, kindly meant message: writing is a labor of paramount seriousness and, if I had any sense, I would not even contemplate it unless impelled by dire need. He phrased his message skillfully, in neutral terms, as if it did not, in fact, concern me, but was more a general message to all hopeful beginners who have no inkling of what they are getting themselves into.

Shortly thereafter, however, he informed me that he himself had also started writing a novel. The solemn tone of his announcement—as if I should feel honored that such precious information had been imparted to me—made it abundantly clear that it would be inappropriate for me to ask him whether he had forgotten his own advice to future writers: it did not, apparently, apply to himself. Unlike the rest of the heedless multitude, my friend, a man well versed in literary matters, knew just what he was doing.

As weeks and months flowed by, I evolved into a sort of accomplice in the creation of his work, though that may be overestimating my role. Perhaps it would be more accurate to say that I was a traveling companion, a mild Doctor Watson upon whom destiny had lavished an unearned favor: to pay with small, technical services for the privilege of dwelling in the company of the great Holmes, while Holmes solved a case of ineffable grandeur and, en passant, threw to his ignorant assistant some crumbs from the ongoing banquet of magisterial skill which was his daily bread.

The technical services were mostly the use of my laser printer, from which emerged chapter after chapter of my friend's novel as soon as each was completed (he, to whom all technology was an odious mystery, refused to purchase anything except the most basic computer, and even that only at my urgent insistence), while in exchange it was my unique gratification (and obligation) to be the first to read them. I also received, direct from the horse's mouth, explanations for whatever seemed to me unclear, as well as for such passages—especially for such passages—which I, in my simplicity, had thought clear enough.

My friend justified this serial enlightenment in terms of a conviction, which grew ever stronger as the novel progressed, that he himself would be the most authoritative—indeed, the only—competent interpreter of his own literary output. He alone would really be able to penetrate all its secrets and perceive every delicate nuance. For a while he even contemplated writing a long critical essay about his own novel, to be published as an afterword to the book itself, though later he dropped that idea and never told me what made him change his mind.

Thus was I given to attend not only the birth of a

work of art, but also the accompanying lectures in literary anatomy, where the holy mystery of creation was, solely for my benefit, revealed to its very marrow, to its ultimate constituent elements. To the atoms of writing, as it were. Related to this was my first introduction to the "Mozart Syndrome."

In a voice subdued almost to a whisper, as befits the conspiratorial revelation of a great secret, my friend informed me of his resemblance to that famous citizen of Salzburg, Austria. Both of them were in possession of that unique, in fact—why not say it?—divine gift whereby the work one wants to create appears in front of one in its entirety, in a great flash, right down to the smallest detail.

Lest I should by any chance think that he immodestly set himself in the same rank with Wolfgang Amadeus—it must be that I carelessly allowed a certain shadow of mild disbelief to pass over my face, although I try hard to keep it totally expressionless during such confessions—my friend hurriedly added the humble qualification that, unlike the great composer, he was most usually hit by such flashes in the most unsuitable surroundings.

For instance, the lightning which announced the arrival of his first novel into the world struck him while he was shaving in his bathroom. And, indeed, he pointed his finger at a small horizontal slash which had not yet completely healed, as the whole thing had happened quite recently. He left open the provenance of five or six other safety-blade slashes on his face—were they, too, the effect of divine inspiration, or merely owing to his well-known clumsiness? In any case, shortly thereafter, my friend stopped shaving; perhaps to reduce the time spent in the undignified surroundings of his bathroom, he grew a beard.

The entire work having been revealed to him in one flash, he—unlike me—was not driven by a reader's impatience to write it down as soon as possible. This was just as well, because he steadfastly adhered to the slowest method of writing invented since the tablet and chisel: he used paper and pencil. (Had he been able to obtain papyrus, I think he would have used that.) As I have mentioned, I somehow managed to persuade him to buy a computer—though, in fact, a dictaphone would have suited him better—but he typed the words into the computer only after he had them down on paper.

He tried to make it look like a part of his ritual of writing, similar to my creation of exactly the right environment, but I think there was another reason: his instinctive distrust of technology. The few appliances that he could not avoid using—geyser, iron, electric heater, hairdryer—in his hands went wrong more often, more comprehensively, and at more awkward moments, than with anyone else. To that were added certain traumatic experiences which he suffered at the very beginning of his computer era.

Having initially installed a simple word-processing program in his machine, I dictated to him some basic instructions for working with it, which he diligently scribbled down. No one will ever know whether his handwriting was, on that occasion, too illegible even for him, or whether he just lost his way among the instructions which to me seemed simplified almost to the point of imbecility; but the very next morning he phoned me to ask how to call up on screen the text (eleven and a half pages) which he had spent much of the previous day writing, carried away by the creative joy of having so swiftly mastered this symbol of modern times.

By means of long and patient questioning, I gleaned from his ever vaguer and more nervous answers, that in all probability he had, after the previous night's work, simply switched off the computer and taken himself blissfully to bed, deeply satisfied with his efforts, having saved not a line of text. Now he was, naturally, angry at himself and no less at the computer, but angriest of all at me; for I had put him up to it. Eleven and a half unrepeatable, unique pages gone with the wind!

He sounded so truly shaken with the realization that, indeed, nothing could be done about it, the text was irretrievably lost, that I had no heart to ask him one cynical question: How could something vanish if it was carved into his mind by divine inspiration? What was lost was, at worst, half a day of typing, which is annoying but hardly a tragedy. He had but to sit at the keyboard again and simply type exactly the same text as yesterday, to the letter, and then be sure to save it.

Although my friend subsequently experienced many other stressful situations with his computer, none were so catastrophic as this first one, mainly because he thereafter adhered strictly to his own rule that, regardless of Mozartian flashes and all the rest, he would first use reliable paper, and only then entrust anything to the fickle memory of a machine.

Most of these minor computer problems arose from my friend's great facility for doing precisely the opposite of what he intended: most commonly, to erase the text he meant to save; then would follow his more or less distraught telephone call from some neighbor's phone at whatever time of day or night he had stopped working, and I would speed as unhesitatingly as an ambulance to his quarter of the city, there to rescue what was recoverable.

Although after the first such intervention I categorically instructed him that, unless he was one hundred percent sure about what to do, he must do nothing whatsoever until I arrived—least of all switch off the computer (unless smoke was billowing out of it)—he quite frequently did switch it off (without any justifying smoke) and was thereafter unable to explain why.

Why, with all that trouble, didn't he give up the computer altogether? Why did he, in this single instance, agree to carry on his martyrdom, bearing this cross of technology, when he had contemptuously rejected every other aspect of it—refusing, for instance, to learn to drive a car although it would have made his life considerably more comfortable, especially as the burden of years became heavier and the public transport system worse *pari passu*; or by refusing to have a telephone, the lack of which had such embarrassing consequences for himself and his neighbors as he invaded their apartments to make calls, usually at awkward hours.

I think the main culprit here was my laser printer. Once his own eyes had verified that, between the moment when he brought me a text saved on diskette to the moment he got the same text printed on paper, faultlessly processed into book format, only a few minutes of time need elapse, it dawned on him that his worst nightmare had ended. For this outcome, he was willing to pay any price: sell his soul to the devil, and even worse—embrace the technology which he otherwise rejected with the contempt of a higher being.

If there was one thing he loathed even more than technology, it was the prospect of collaborating with publishers' copy editors, typists and proofreaders. The first of the three species, copy editors, dared to desecrate, by their amateurish half-knowledge, the faultless sanctity of his text. That their intentions were benign did nothing to justify their unhallowed deeds. Quite the contrary; he experienced any intervention of theirs as a physical wound. It sometimes happened that an intervention was indeed inappropriate, because the copy editor failed to understand the context; but, mostly, they were grammatical corrections, and proper beyond any possibility of debate, because they were backed up by the official Grammar and Orthography of our language.

The trouble with that was that my friend only partially, and conditionally, accepted the authority of the Grammar and Orthography, for he regarded many of the compilers of those documents as dullards and jackasses. There was no easy way to resolve such situations, because the Grammar and Orthography were the Law and the Prophets to the copy editors, who refused to budge from the laid-down norms even when they privately agreed with my friend that some of the official formulae might not be the most fortunate.

But his troubles with copy editors were moderate, cerebral differences of opinion next to those that arose from the joint actions of typists and proofreaders. My friend was aware that those who type manuscripts inevitably make a number of errors (and he was especially grieved by the multitudes of words incorrectly divided between syllables at the ends of lines), and equally aware that such errors might slip by proofreaders (one of whom once responded to an angry rebuke from the professor with the hesitant remark that there would be fewer such occurrences if the professor did not have such a difficult vocabulary, and especially if he made his paragraphs shorter), and so he demanded to be the last living soul to read the galleys immediately prior to printing; but even that was no help.

The printed books simply crawled with typos. Some mistakes were so glaring that the simplest explanation was that he himself was grossly inept as a proofreader—he simply had no eye for it—and one must also bear in mind that he was reading his own text. But my friend rejected this interpretation, although it would be clearly in the spirit of Occam's Razor, which, in other matters, he frequently invoked. Nobody could convince him that these errors did not spring from a conspiracy, calculated to harm his text as much as possible.

Typists and proofreaders, he propounded, opening his soul to me on one occasion, deliberately make the sort of errors which will be hard to spot. How else to explain the fact that in all forty-three places in his latest book where he intended the dignified word "drevni" (ancient) to appear, they had printed the banal "drveni" (wooden)? And on eleven of those forty-three occasions, the word was at the end of a line and divided into syllables incorrectly. All of which was, of course, discovered only after the book was in the bookshops.

After these traumatic experiences, which colored a good first half of my friend's creative life, it is clear why the transition to electronic book-publishing was, for him, a gift from Heaven. All of a sudden, no more copy editors! No more typists, not a single proofreader in sight! The nightmare was dispelled by the diskette, on which he could record whatever he liked, without the nauseating obligation of arguing subsequently with some incompetent individual about what might or might not be stated just so; better still, no more living in terror that malevolent gremlins would deliberately sabotage his work. The headaches the machine cost him were trivial in the glorious light of these benefits.

As I had played a key part in his cyber-enlightenment, and as the services of my laser printer were always at his disposal, he found it appropriate, as a man of breeding, somehow to express his gratitude. Recently made aware of my fond wish to launch myself, also, into the adventure of writing, but, naturally, disapproving of it ("there must be some sense and order in things, these matters are, as is well known, serious, we cannot all do everything, *quod licet Iovi . . .*"), he decided, as the most competent authority, to soften his stance and to admit me, despite all my faults and his own misgivings, into the realm of Literature, but only to the limited extent which he considered justified.

He introduced me as a character in his novel.

I appeared infrequently, apart from which it was strictly forbidden that I recognize myself, so I was allowed no opportunity to take public pride at having finally entered World Literature. The ban was based on the principle that any prose character exists independently of their real-life model, which is fine from the standpoint of literary theory, no doubt, but I have a faint suspicion that there was more to it in this case. Had my friend allowed me to recognize myself publicly, and thus gratify my vanity—and what would that have cost him, anyway?—it would have set a precedent, which might lead to many other recognitions, especially among the principal characters, and that was definitely to be avoided.

With this in mind, I was ordered explicitly and from the start that when I read his novel it must be from the standpoint of an amnesiac, so as to reduce to a minimum the danger of any such recognition. My attention was drawn to the axiom that only such virginal reading, unburdened by any unwelcome comparisons with reality, might be regarded as a proper reading.

To fulfill this requirement I acted as dumb as I could, but with only patchy success. I managed more or less not to know the things I knew of the two main characters, but my memory persistently refused to betray me when my own persona appeared on the stage of the novel. What blew the whole thing sky-high was not my friend's decision that in his novel only I, of all the characters based on real models, should appear under my actual name; rather, it was the genitive form of the possessive pronoun which was almost always attached to it in that context: the pronoun "our."

Although many people are unaware of it, "our" is no ordinary possessive pronoun. In fact it amounts to a title, and a title not easily won. Almost equivalent to a knighthood, one might say, albeit not one granted by a king. The title "our" is conferred by socially prominent families in our town; the individuals who receive that honor, after many years of devoted service, are particularly hardworking and loyal menials and servants, errand-boys, butlers, housekeepers, gardeners and in general those who free the distinguished family from dirty, manual, technical—in a word, unbecoming work.

To become "our," which denotes the highest possible degree of intimacy between the upper and the lower level of society (and that means reaching the borderline of caste separation, a line that can never be crossed), you have to be always at hand, for a very long time, whenever there is a blown fuse or lightbulb to be replaced, a drain to be unclogged, a stove hotplate to be fixed, linoleum to be glued to the kitchen floor, sagging bookshelves to be firmed up, a picture to be taken to the framer's shop—or when computer glitches need to be sorted out.

The services of a chauffeur are also highly valued. No wonder: would a serious person squander time on such trivialities as learning to drive, or buying and maintaining a car, when that same time could be applied so much more graciously, for instance to reading the collected works of Immanuel Kant? (An extremely chic occupation in the most respected strata of the upper classes.)

In my friend's novel I retained my real name, and even filled a role similar to what he presumably imagines my real role to be, but only his skillful use of the possessive genitive "our" conveyed the full literary depth of my character. Marginal though I was, in this one respect I managed to outshine all the other characters, even the protagonist, because none of them, despite the author's utmost efforts, received such a delicately nuanced linguistic treatment. It is a marvel what can be achieved with only three letters.

If the character in which I, without permission, recognized myself had not been so successful, it is unlikely that I would have been quite so hurt by that final, written confirmation of how I appear in the eyes of my friend. I would have glided coolly over the entire matter, and would even have felt superior—telling myself that it was just the caricature I had expected—but in the circumstances such composure was impossible.

Although I did what I could to curtail its corrosive effect on my psyche, my injured vanity soon started to influence my behavior towards my friend. He, of course, had no idea what lay behind my increasing tendency to do things which we both knew upset or unnerved him. As I have mentioned, I had sometimes done such things before, perversely enjoying his rage, but only under extreme provocation; now the smallest matter would serve to raise my hackles.

Such as when he popped in for a visit unannounced.

That was, in any case, his usual habit, derived from his firm belief that he was doing me a great favor by condescending to spend time in my company—and not for short periods, either. Such paratroop raids on my time were not invariably welcome; indeed, he often interrupted me in the course of work that could not be postponed; but he did not notice—or chose not to notice—the embarrassment which he so often caused me. I myself was inhibited by my wish to be a considerate host, which restrained me from telling him openly how I felt; and as for my other signals, more delicate but nonetheless clear to anyone of normal sensitivity—he was deaf and blind.

Yesterday, all unannounced, he spoke from the intercom, stating his name briefly, as if it were a password good at every door. The occasion was the most inopportune yet. On that very day, at that precise time, after many sterile weeks, I had sat down once again at the computer, enjoying that increase of tension which intimates that something new is about to start flowing out of the darkness whence springs my prose. I hoped it might be the long-delayed closing chapter; it was really high time to complete the project, be it a novel or a collection of stories. The ambience was faultless at last: through the lowered slats the afternoon sun, by now invisible, was sending painfully strong blue light in thin streaks.

As my frustration was unavoidable, it was inevitable that I should react in some way. If I was to be denied this opportunity to write, at least we would discover, once and for all, why that process should differ so much between my case and his. Indeed, could there be any contrast stronger than a Mozartian flash against an impenetrable darkness? I therefore mentioned the darkness to him, expecting him to reject it instantly with one of his displays of livid rage. But none emerged; instead, and quite unexpectedly, I was awarded that superior psychiatric séance, concluding with the catastrophic words, "And this will be of some use."

Without that diagnosis, nothing would have happened. My initial anger had already ebbed, mollified by his ridiculous questions that I had answered in suitably ridiculous terms. Now it flared up again, and I, blinded by its glare, decided to go one step beyond the rational, to a place I had never taken anyone before— to the far shore, the other side of the darkness. I had to punish him somehow, and if this failed to enrage him, nothing would.

It had to be presented as science fiction for maximum emotional impact, his loathing for that genre going far beyond the ordinary. He despised many aspects of literature (he despised all literature in fact, except a few favored authors—coincidentally, those whose books only he was competent to interpret, like his own), but he could, in rare moments of relative benevolence, find the odd extenuating circumstance for a few genres and authors; for science fiction, never. He did not tolerate SF in any form, not even the parodic, which (subject to a number of rigid constraints) he regarded as the only permissible approach to genre literature.

For a long time I had attributed this to his naive prejudice (born of his disgusted refusal ever to open any work of that sort) that SF consisted exclusively of gauche and unreserved praise of the technology for which his own general distaste was so well known—the computer being the exception which tested, and on this occasion confirmed, the rule. But after many hours squandered in bitter and utterly fruitless debate with him about this, I perceived that there must be something more to it. He was not bothered by SF as such; he could have dismissed it with a single glance, one of his well-practiced expressions of supercilious disdain would have sufficed.

What really bothered him, apparently, was my intimacy with the genre. By seizing every opportunity to denigrate science fiction, mostly without any provocation, he was in fact, for reasons most noble and friendly, struggling to save my blundering soul. Sometimes he did it with the softness of a missionary, sometimes with the cruelty of the Inquisition, though (to judge by the inexorable and fervent passion that then possessed him) he preferred the latter mode. His orthodox crusade for my salvation from the pestilence of SF gradually grew into a real obsession, which showed in his rhetoric; he would open almost any discussion of the genre with his adaptation of Cato: "Science fiction delendum est!"

Now was the hour for SF to strike back.

There is nothing whatsoever creative in the act of writing, I stated as my opening shot. It was calculated to anger him enormously, but my conscience was clear; he had brought it on himself. *There are no flashes, and no godly trances.*

(He started to blink at that, as he usually does when something rubs him up the wrong way.)

There is only the darkness which yawns between the worlds—between this, our world, and multitudes of oth-

ers, some very similar and some totally different. Some monotonously ordinary, and some unthinkably strange. To say of these worlds that they are far from us would be incorrect, because the darkness which separates us is neither space nor time. They are neither near nor far, neither before nor after. They are beyond.

(Here he used his index finger to loosen the knot on his tie. It was of a garish green background, embellished, near the lower end, with several small spots of mustard, egg and gravy, almost invisible in a pattern of similar color.)

Only those who have the Sight may look through that darkness. But even among them, not all share the ability. Some see better, some worse; some notice many details, others can barely make out the contours of the most salient landmarks. For this reason the reports of what has been seen vary markedly. There are good reports, and poor reports; some report detail, some general outlines. Yet none of it is invented or created. There is no invention, only testimony. No creation, only mediation.

(At this point a sound escaped from the bottom of his throat; it was supposed to be a mere clearing, a controlled little cough, but it emerged more like a death rattle.)

On that other side, there are also some with the Sight. They, too, can penetrate through the darkness, and see another world: our world. And all the worlds which are separated from us only by space and time. Worlds ordinary and worlds miraculous. Some of those who see us think, in their pride and vanity, that we are a mere figment of their own minds. Others, whose devotion is more ardent, more selfless and more pure, know that we were not created in their "heads," that we are as real as they.

(He started to wriggle in the armchair, crossing and uncrossing his legs, left over right, right over left. The shoe on the upper leg would, in the process, hang momentarily over the glass slab of my small coffee table where I keep a ceramic vase. It looked out of place there, partly because it was so tattered and dirty, but mainly because both the shoelaces were wrongly threaded through the little metal-reinforced holes, so that they barely tied at the top.)

Nothing save the Sight has managed to pierce the darkness so far, and many, both here and there, believe that things can never be otherwise—that only the ethereal Sight may cross the cobweb bridge which connects the worlds. Few are the persistent ones, on both sides, to whom the impossible is just another word for challenge. The daring who will, imprudently, reach for the ungraspable, the unreasonable who will without consideration chase the uncatchable, the heroes who dash madly for the unattainable. Their curse is immeasurable, but also immeasurable is their glory.

Judging by the flustered flush suffusing his face, an explosion was imminent, but, to my surprise and disappointment, none occurred. For several long minutes he sat there in deep silence, his mouth shut though he was breathing deeply as he gazed at me over his glasses without blinking. Then his head started to sway left and right. When, finally, he did speak, it was in a trembling voice, which showed that the storm within had not yet subsided completely. "How would you like to lie down on the couch one more time, for a little while, hm?" he proposed.

I lay flat on the couch, almost repentantly, perceiving how wrong I had been. I had never before told anybody anything about the darkness, the Sight, the worlds, and the rest, so I had no standards of comparison. The expected reaction seemed to have aborted because I had gone too far: as I had recounted it, the story must have been a little too rich even for a man with a far smaller burden of prejudices than his. To him it must have seemed a clear and simple confirmation that I was seriously deranged. That diagnosis helped him to quell his anger.

We commenced another psychoanalytical séance, but he took no notes on this occasion—he needed none. Indeed, it was only for the sake of form that my self-appointed shrink needed to ask any questions, for everything was already clear to him. He merely seized on the chance to display his great and enviable skill in formulating astute questions. He pressed his finger-tips together and rested his chin on the summit thus created, in the manner favored by the most searching questioners. And on he went.

Did I find pleasure in watching fish copulate in my aquarium?

I doubted that I would recognize what they were doing. Ichthyology is not my forte. In any case, the aquarium, while I had one, was to me more an arena of premature death than one for creating life, the domain of Thanatos, not Eros. That was why I had given it up, despite my delight in the wild, exotic beauty of its tiny residents. It was enough to make a single little mistake—forget to feed them, for instance, or wrongly adjust the thermostat and the air pump—and mass extinction followed. The cactuses which now reside in the ex-aquarium are no less beautiful, but far less demanding, and their lives are far less fragile.

Did I frequently experience an erection in an airplane during takeoff?

Of course not, because I very rarely travel by air, and when I do my terror is directly proportional to the altitude which we have attained—no basis for sexual excitement. If there is any eroticism in flying, it could only be in the appearance of clouds seen from above. These look so . . . sleepy, intoxicating.

Would I rather make love to a hedgehog or a stork?

Not much of a choice. My suspicion is that both would be exceedingly painful. But if one must follow such a line of speculation, why not take it to the limit? Turning towards the armchair, I confided that the ultimate sexual experience of a *ménage á trois* with one of each would suit me best. I did so with some diffidence, but that was immediately dispelled by his brief, insight-laden smile.

Did I ever dream that a computer was attempting to molest me?

No need to dream: I frequently had that impression while fully awake, when (mainly in response to my mistakes, but sometimes through whims of its own) it started to act in an unpredictable, capricious manner. But on such occasions I had no one to call for help; I had only my own ingenuity and patience to rely on. Yet the question was not entirely vacuous: yes, the computer did sometimes slink into my dreams, although for reasons of my own I was not prepared to give my friend any details lest he become even more firmly convinced that something was wrong with me, though it certainly was nothing to do with molestation. . . .

After several more questions in the same spirit, when the time for the verdict arrived, I expected nothing good. My answers had, obviously, confirmed the conclusion which had been present from the start. He gave me the gaze which he normally reserves for those occasions when he is about to flunk some good-looking co-ed. A gaze so eloquent, that in fact he had no need to add the words: "When will you shake off that science-fictional . . . childishness? See where it has brought you." I sat up on the couch and closed my eyes. I started to rub my forehead, just above my nose. The dull drumming which had started there told me for certain that I had reached the limit of my endurance. From its outset the whole exercise had been devoid of any meaning or purpose except to afford me a modicum of rather perverse entertainment, but now it was time to end the show.

The afternoon had long since melted into evening, made yet darker by the blind, which was still down.

The only illumination in my study was the ghostly gray radiance from the computer screen—the monitor on which I had been prevented from typing a single word. The frustration was overwhelming—not that the flow from the darkness had ceased; the tension was still there, and perhaps I could yet give it rein, if only allowed the chance. But I was to be allowed no chance.

Before his visit was finally concluded, two hours and thirty five minutes later, my friend first regaled me with an extended lecture on the history of entelechy; delivered a detailed account (with commentary) of an anecdote from the seventh or eighth volume of the diary of his favorite writer; colorfully retold the story of a bizarre event from his childhood involving a huge, vicious dog that I had heard at least ten times before; reported to me with damning exegesis the most unseemly intrigues now convulsing the Faculty, and at the very end—the dessert comes last—he told me of his new literary undertaking, which was, in fact, the main reason for his visit.

He announced it in a becomingly dignified tone. Thus I learned that, very recently, his second novel had come to him, as had the first, in a single flash of enlightenment; this time, though, not in the bathroom during shaving, but in an even more awkward place: in the basement of his apartment building, where, in his absentmindedness, he had ended up by mistake.

Lest I suffer any unnecessary anxiety, I was immediately told, unambiguously and with a bountiful smile, that on this occasion also I would enjoy all the benefits I had previously been granted: I would be allowed to utilize my laser printer without hesitation, I would retain the exclusive right to read each fresh chapter before anyone else, and to have everything clarified to me firsthand. Finally, as though as an afterthought, he added, with a mildly menacing motion of his finger, that the ban on any inopportune recognition would not, of course, be lifted.

By the time he finally left—forgetting to take with him not only the page from the notepad with the coded shrink's notes, but also his reading glasses—the drumming from above my nose had spread throughout my head. It was particularly sharp at the base of my skull where it joins the neck; I kept massaging the place with one hand, but the great splotch of pain at anchor there refused to sail away. My many years of experience with migraine told me ineluctably that the critical point had been passed: no medicine could help me now. All I could do for myself in that condition was to lie down, close my eyes and hope for the blessed deliverance of sleep. . . .

Which did arrive, but only after I had passed through torment. The epicenter of pain moved around, mercilessly and successively crushing my sinuses, my temples, my forehead and the back of my head. The hardest to bear was when it hit the base of my eye sockets; I felt as if a red-hot iron were burrowing from the inside, seeking to goad my eyeballs into popping out to escape the searing heat.

This bodily infirmity inevitably brought on a deep depression. I sank into a reverie over the many opportunities that my life had once afforded, and now were missed or wasted—either way, gone irretrievably. I tried to grope my way towards the darkness, to invoke it, but now there was only the mere absence of natural light, punched through with numerous, multi-colored flashes of headache. I had lost the connection that I had awaited so long; the link was severed, leaving behind a mute emptiness. All lost, ruined—and for what?

As if in answer to that question, fragments of the evening's conversation started to drift back: frozen images which would briefly emerge from the abyss of memory, only to plunge back into it and dissipate into nonexistence. Their swift succession had a hypnotic, sedative effect on me; too gradually to notice, the pain retreated into the background, then evaporated. And just as surreptitiously, while I was intent on the unreal lights flowing across my inner eyelids, I fell asleep.

In dreams the show continued, but now the images came to life. There was a woman without a face; she was trying to feed me with milk from her vast, swollen breast, yet I somehow knew that she was not my mother; milk spurted all over my face from that udder, on which the branching network of veins was clearly visible; milk painted my face green and trickled down my chin, but I kept my mouth firmly shut, fearing that it might be snake venom.

The breast was replaced by a night pot, also unnaturally enlarged, which levitated above my head and bobbed about, as if shaken by violent waves. It was obvious that the contents might at any moment fall on my head unless I could find shelter; I looked around urgently, but I could see only a boulder of some sort; closer observation revealed that it was a marble statue of an index finger upraised in warning. The finger began to sway and totter, with a harsh screeching sound, and this caused a current of air which finally overturned the yellow chamber pot.

Instinctively I raised my arms over my head, but they were inadequate protection against a heavy shower of shiny letters which splashed down on me. The letters varied in size and color, and the porous styrofoam of which they were all made had a mild, sweetish fragrance, like that of fruit tea. The shower increased to a waterfall, and soon I was waist-deep in this alphabetic flood, then shoulder-deep. It was like standing helpless in a grain silo, while tons of wheat cascaded down.

Once the letters covered my head I began to choke. In panic, I reached up with both hands to swim for the surface, but instead of emerging from the sea of letters,

I merely slid up and out of an item of clothing which, after I had somehow struggled out and grabbed some air, I realized was more appropriate to a woman: a lady's formal evening dress, in turquoise brocade, sleeveless, and cut low in the back.

I hardly had time to ask myself how I came to be wearing such a thing, before I was horrified to discover that I had on further female apparel under it: a two-piece suit in dark red, consisting of jacket and skirt—such as airline stewardesses often wear. I quickly struggled out of that as well, but my torment was by no means ended thereby. Underneath the jacket was an airy, light, flouncy, summer dress. It had a flowery pattern in dark violet which I seemed to know from somewhere; while pulling it off over my head, hands trembling, I recognized it from the couch in my study.

The fashion show went on and on: after the light dress there were black trousers, also of flimsy material, with very narrow legs which barely covered my calves, teamed with a bright silk blouse. Thereafter came a crinoline in heavy brocade supported on a thick wire grid; tight blue jeans and a cotton gingham shirt; a blue kimono, its back completely covered by an embroidered dragon; tight, bottle-green corduroy trousers and a canary-yellow, turtleneck sweater in lambswool.

Struggling out of each layer, I moved at an ever more neurotic tempo. There seemed to be no end to my capacity for female clothing, even though I never seemed at all overdressed. But, when the first hint of an end appeared, I greeted it not with relief but with panic. I pulled myself out of an old-fashioned, floor-length gown with a tight bodice (which was wrongly laced), to find myself clad only in a petticoat.

I managed, with some difficulty, to overcome the momentum of my frenetic stripping, afraid of what I might find underneath. For several moments I stood still, torn by conflicting drives: the urge to rid myself of the petticoat, which I definitely had no business wearing, and the wish to leave it on so as not to face the terrifying certainty of switched gender. But this unstable balance could not endure for long: with slow, hesitant moves I finally slid the straps from my shoulders, and the silky petticoat flowed off.

It revealed no body, male or female. There was, in fact, no body to reveal. A form, of sorts, yes; remotely body-like, but definitely not human, and perfectly transparent. I gazed unblinkingly down at a most unusual aquarium, where a varied population of little fishes darted among tiny cactuses.

I barely had time to marvel before the perfectly limpid water of the brick-shaped yard-long aquarium was suddenly made turbid by a thick redness gushing up from the bottom. Before this bloody haze completely blocked my view, I saw the fishes swimming madly to impale themselves on the cactus needles. The long, thin daggers penetrated their bodies and re-emerged, but the red liquid was not their blood—it spurted from the tips of the daggers themselves, which trembled lasciviously with each emission.

I felt myself partaking of their bliss, as if I were collecting some sort of rent from the tenants who had chosen to celebrate this orgiastic spree of death in my bizarrely altered torso. But it was not my destiny to share their climax; a large stork suddenly materialized beside the aquarium, a tall bird wearing thick-rimmed glasses (their rims repaired in several places with brittle old sticky tape), and a worn-out, mustard-colored necktie. She (for I regarded the stork as female) stood next to the aquarium for a few moments, shaking her head in obvious disapproval and disgust, then with a single, violent stabbing motion, drove her thick beak through the wall of glass.

I experienced a sharp pain, as if a sword had been driven into my vitals. I opened my mouth to yell, but no sound emerged; in mute agony, I looked on help-lessly while the pinkish, gluey contents of the aquarium slowly oozed round the stork's legs. But when the last of the fluid had trickled out to expose the bottom there was no sign of what ought to have been there. No detumescent cactuses, no fishes impaled thereon: only a multitude of sponges, trembling gelatinously, newly and obviously swollen with what they had absorbed.

The stork bent down to press the sponges caressing-ly with her beak. She did not do it randomly but in meticulous order, and the pressed sponges did not release dirty water, as I for some reason had assumed they would. Quite the contrary, small sea urchins covered with slime emerged from them. In color they ranged from a darkish yellow to almost black, and they made tiny sounds similar to the peeping of chicks.

Having coaxed them all out, the stork raised her head, turned her beak up, opened it, and uttered a clear, metallic gong-like sound, which to the prickly chicks was, undoubtedly, a signal to leave the site of their entry into the world. As soon as they made their way across the bottom of the aquarium and between the glass shards around it, each one achieved a meta-morphosis: they changed from sea urchins into common hedgehogs, large, completely black, and covered with a forest of long, bristling spines.

The stork turned away from me and slowly walked into the distance, while the hedgehogs formed up into two separate rows or columns behind her. Once the formation was complete, the stork flapped her wings and took off, folding her legs under her body. I was not greatly surprised when the hedgehogs also took off, maintaining perfect formation; nor did it seem odd when I, too, rose up to fly at the rear of the squad-ron. But I was completely baffled by the fact that fly-ing in this insubstantial, invisible airplane, with an ever-deeper abyss beneath my feet, didn't frighten me.

On the contrary, I felt light-headed, almost drunk with joy, and thrilled with the experience.

I soon got the vague impression that this excitement was becoming palpable, swollen. Suddenly embarrassed I looked down, but there was nothing to be seen: I still had no torso. Perplexed, I raised my eyes—and noticed that I was alone in the air. No stork before me, no hedgehogs, no invisible airplane. Nothing. Just a vast shimmering grayness into which I stared dully.

Then, before fear could take possession of me—which would undoubtedly lead to a headlong plunge—I realized what the shimmering was: a colossal computer screen, filling the entire heavens in front of me. Nothing was written on it, but that did not worry me. I knew, with the complete certainty typical of dreams, that words would very shortly appear on that screen; huge words, shining as bright as the Revelation itself, words which would flow not from my head, but from the darkness, across the cobweb-thin bridge, from the other side.

Unless . . .

Unless a sound came.

And, inevitably, there was a sound.

Very quiet at first, soft as the last buzzings of a dying insect lying slumped beneath the impenetrable obstacle of a distant windowpane. It rapidly rose to a muted roar, the purring of the well-tuned engine of a limousine driven by a white-gloved chauffeur, with Immanuel Kant himself sitting in the rear, reading his own Complete Works. That in turn was modified into the silvery tinkling of a small bell on a salver, of the sort used in the mansions of the rich to summon a liveried footman.

Of course, I had to respond, there was no way of backing off from that obligation.

My eyes still closed, I extended a hand and gropingly found the phone on the bedside table. Before lift-

ing the receiver and croaking out a drowsy "Hello?" I
opened one eye and observed the large red numerals on
the alarm clock's display: 06:14. Instantly the base of
my skull began to throb.

It was he, of course. I did not wait to hear any questions; instead, I gave him two affirmative answers right
off: yes, he had forgotten his glasses at my place, and
yes, he could come and get them. Yes, I was already
awake. No, no, it was by no means too early. Oh you
don't say? You had to wake him up to make this call?
Well what sort of a neighbor is it, in God's name, who
is still asleep at this time of day! Unheard of! I know
you cannot work without them. Yes, a new novel, you
told me. No, I am not going into your part of town
today, unfortunately, but I'll be at home. All day, yes.
Good.

While I went through my morning routine, the
splotch of pain resumed its progress through my skull.
But it was not as blinding as on the previous night: now
it produced only muffled flashes which hit me mainly
in the region above the eyebrows. I stayed in the shower for longer than usual. Thin sharp jets of warm water
gradually leached the pressure from my head, but it returned as soon as I started toweling myself dry in front
of the clouded mirror, surrounded by a mist of warm
steam and ethereal bathroom smells.

The pain finally disappeared only after I had drunk
a large cup of strong, hot tea. It was some English mix,
of uncertain origin, and it smelled simultaneously of
fir trees and dog rose. The tea was more black than
brown, even after I squeezed into it one-half of a juicy,
thick-skinned lemon. I felt the effects of the mixture
almost instantly, as if I had introduced it directly into
my bloodstream, not through my stomach.

The blind: I pulled it down slowly, ritually. Its shadow, sliding over my face exposed to the heat of the
morning sun, seemed to switch off some great electric

heater. Today would, again, be unbearably hot; once again I anticipated a visit which might last for quite a while, although its ostensible reason didn't seem to justify a prolonged stay; and the beneficial effects of the tea would pass sooner or later, which would assuredly bring on a return of the headache. Each one of these three circumstances would be, in itself, sufficient to shatter the perfection of the ambience, so I could afford no further delay.

I switched on the computer.

The Ghostwriter

Had the email started any other way, I certainly would have deleted it immediately. For a long time I have saved almost every message and replied to most of them, but finally I came to my senses. Now I only save the ones that seem important because there is less and less time. But what writer could resist the flattery of a devotee, even an anonymous one?

Highly Esteemed Writer,

I am a great fan of your work. I have a business proposal to make in this regard. Would you be interested in hearing about it?

Sincerely,
An Admirer

I opened a new folder, called it "Admirer" and saved the email as "Admirer 001". I did not expect the number of messages I exchanged with this unknown Admirer to have three digits, but that is how I have standardized my email archive. Every name starts with "001". Not many of them have reached "010". Only in correspondence with several friends is the first number greater than zero.

I am so close to "999" with one of them that I will soon have to change to four-digit numbers. In order to keep the archive standardized, all the others will have another zero tacked onto the front. Even using a convenient file-renaming program, the work will take the better part of two days. I was recently amazed to find out that over the years I have collected more than 6,300 emails in 417 folders. But there are no shortcuts when you are a neatness freak. I have yet to come to my senses in that regard and it is not certain I ever will.

Admirer's email address did not reveal a thing: *admirer@gmail.com*. He had evidently chosen it in order to say as little as possible about himself. It was even likely that he used it solely to write to me. Let's just see how important it is to him to keep his identity secret, I thought.

Esteemed Admirer,

The only way I might be interested in hearing your proposal is if I know who is behind it. I am not in the habit of getting involved with people if I don't know their name, despite their being "a great fan of my work".

Sincerely,
Writer

Two and a half minutes later there was another gong from the three speakers placed on the wide, varnished board above my desk between the radiator and the window. Ever since the computer started informing me of incoming mail this way, my life has become much easier. Before that, I felt like I had a telephone without a ring, so I had to pick up the receiver from time to time to check whether someone was calling me.

Even though I knew the analogy did not work—I could miss a call from a silent phone, while the email would wait for me permanently in my virtual mailbox—I interrupted what I was doing more and more often to check whether something had come in. I told myself that I was being absurd—to say nothing of the time I wasted and lack of concentration on my work—

but when has a sober inner voice brought anyone to their senses?

And just when impatience was gaining serious momentum, forcing me to check my mail at nearly three-minute intervals, my email-telephone acquired a ring. I found by chance that I could give my incoming email an alert tone. This did not put reason completely back in charge. I keep the speakers turned up way too high so that I can hear them when I'm not in my study. If I am in it, and that's where I spend most of my time, I not only jump at every gong but sometimes—especially when engrossed in writing—hop off my chair. Moreover, when a long time passes without any gong, I succumb to temptation and check whether a message has arrived, persuading myself that computers, just like people, can sometimes fail, although not once have I ever found any unannounced email.

Highly Esteemed Writer,

Unfortunately, I cannot reveal my identity. You will understand why if you let me make my proposal. You have nothing to lose by hearing it. Should you find it unacceptable, I will annoy you no further.

Sincerely,
Admirer

I stared through the drooping leaves of the yucca quivering in the imperceptible currents of air. The large round brass flowerpot stands between the middle and right speaker. The interlacing greenery partially blocks my view, but it also breaks the uniform blue of the morning sky that fills the window. My bleary eyes wander that way whenever I'm collecting my thoughts as I write.

Admirer was right. I had nothing to lose by letting

him make his proposal. Actually, he could have done it already. But he didn't want to without my permission. I would have to find a fitting response to this courtesy, even if I didn't know who was behind it. In any case, he was clearly not some country bumpkin. Language is a telling indication about people. This person was accustomed to polite manners. Even two short messages were enough to demonstrate that.

Furthermore, I wanted to hear the sound of the gong. I receive the fewest emails during the summer and this certainly does not suit the addict, even partially recovered, that I have become. Here was a chance to ease the drought. For want of anything better, even a short exchange with a stranger would be welcome. There was no fear that this would interrupt my work. I was not exactly inundated there either.

Esteemed Admirer,

I await your proposal.

Sincerely,
Writer

In less than a minute, the gong sounded again.

Highly Esteemed Writer,

Thank you for being so obliging!
My proposal is simple. Would you be willing to write a novel for me?

Sincerely,
Admirer

I couldn't be as fast as Admirer. Unlike me, he clearly did not waste time archiving our correspondence.

He would probably do it later. If he truly was what he claimed, it was unlikely that he would simply erase an email from a writer whose work he admired. Perhaps I too could have put off saving it for later, but habit won out. In any case, I wasn't in any hurry.

Esteemed Admirer,

I'm not sure that I understand. What do you mean exactly by "write a novel for me"? Dedicate my next book to you?

Sincerely,
Writer

Soon after I sent the message, I remembered that I was in a hurry after all. I got up from the desk and scurried into the kitchen. The tea was probably lukewarm by now. Preoccupied with writing to Admirer, it had been the farthest thing from my mind. In order to avoid taking all the paraphernalia into my study— the teaspoon, the saucer for the used teabag, the small pitcher of freshly squeezed lemon juice, the round glass bowl with brown sugar—I leave my cup on the cold burner of my small stove and finish preparing my tea after it has properly cooled.

The best time to add the lemon and sugar is when the brown liquid has just stopped steaming and a film has yet to form on the surface. This happens between the eleventh and thirteenth minute. The problem, however, is that I have more and more trouble getting there on time. And if I'm late, the tea is not only too cold but lacking in flavor. After eighteen minutes all I can do is pour it down the drain. In spite of the fact that many people like ice-cold tea, particularly during the summer, I consider it a sacrilege. If tea isn't hot, it isn't tea.

Just as I entered the kitchen, the gong sounded from my study. I stopped briefly, hesitating. Curiosity urged me to go back to my computer, but it might not be too late to save the tea. I glanced at the cup. It was no longer steaming and a film had started to form. I was unable to judge when I had poured boiling water into the cup, but even if it was a quarter of an hour ago, most of the taste would be preserved. I went up to the stove. This was more important, after all. Furthermore, if Admirer got the impression that I had nothing better to do than correspond with him, my reputation would be adversely affected. Let him wait a bit.

I took a sip of tea on my way back to my desk. About sixty-five percent of its best characteristics had been preserved. The lemon's tartness eclipsed some of the green tea's delicate taste, which would not have happened if it were a little warmer. Well, all right, it could have been worse. Just a minute or two later and it would have tasted like flat lemonade.

I moved the mouse a bit to get rid of the screensaver, took another sip of tea from the cup and then looked at Admirer's new message.

Highly Esteemed Writer,

Please excuse me for not making myself clear. I was not thinking of a dedication. What I had in mind was for you to write a novel and then turn over the authorship rights to me.

Sincerely,
Admirer

Squinting as I do when something bewilders me, I reread the short message. My fingers were already heading for the keyboard to reply, when Felix jumped on my desk and got in the way. As I was coming back with the tea a moment before, he had been lying on the two-seater, apparently sound asleep, snoring like he always does when he sleeps on his back. His forepaws were bent and his back paws stretched out. I hadn't noticed that the snoring had stopped and did not hear him get up and come towards me. Although he has acquired many human characteristics after living with me for so long, he has not lost all his feline traits. His movements, for example, are still effectively silent.

I brought Felix home from my customary walk along the river two years, nine months and thirteen days ago. A starving and terrified kitten emerged from under a bush in front of me, mewing softly. What else could I do but take him with me? Had I wanted a cat, however, I would have chosen another one. Felix is a mixed-breed calico with lopsided ears, eyes that are always full of sleep and a stubby tail. He has rather a homely look about him. It took weeks before I finally got rid of his fleas.

Felix had an easier time getting used to me than I to him. It is not hard to get accustomed to comfort. It took a great deal of patience, however, for me to take on the duties that come with sharing my living space. Only when I had completely accepted Felix as a member of the household did I realize that he had come in the nick of time. Soon I would have become a hopeless loner who could not stand to have anyone near him.

Felix has become oddly involved in my writing. Ever since he was little he has jumped on my desk as soon as I sit down at it in the morning. Even though there is enough empty space to lie down, at first he stretched out on the keyboard. I would wait in frustration until he condescended to move so I could start writing. This would take quite some time but I, of course, could certainly not move him. That would be bullying and how could I be a bully, particularly towards my nearest and dearest?

I discovered why Felix did it by accident. He wanted his morning share of affection. As soon as I had petted him for a few minutes, he would get off the keyboard and lie down next to it, letting me write. Over time, this turned into a morning ritual. If for some reason Felix did not appear on the keyboard, I would immediately think that he was ailing. Following the vet's instructions, I would feel the tips of his ears to make sure he didn't have a temperature.

Soon I came to value Felix's company on my desk while I was writing. If he isn't there, everything grinds to a halt. I agonize over details, the plot goes astray or I even start doubting the point of what I'm working on. And vice versa. When he is next to me, everything goes smoothly. One day I will have to find a way to repay him for being almost a co-author. The least I can do is dedicate a book to him. What do I care if it shocks some literary purist?

When I bought a laptop four and a half months ago, Felix fell in love with it at his very first sniff. Now he passes by the keyboard in the morning with total indifference and lies on top of the little computer that I keep on my desk, even though I rarely use it. He dozes on top of it even after his petting.

Since it does not interfere with my work, this would not bother me if it weren't for Felix's weight. Burdened by a life of comfort, the once scrawny little kitten has grown into a large tomcat, to put it mildly. I feared for the poor laptop under him, but I did not remove Felix from there either. And I could not put the laptop somewhere else. Felix would have been terribly disappointed not to see it on my desk.

Actually, there was no real need to buy this second computer. I succumbed to a panic attack after a three and a half-hour power cut. This actually happens very rarely, but since I had been caught up in a whirlwind of writing at the time, I decided not to allow it to happen again. I was haunted by the thought of all I might have failed to write during the blackout. Some moments can never be repeated.

As I was coming back from the store with my new laptop, I had a brief pang of conscience. I reproached myself for needlessly wasting money when there was a much simpler way to solve the problem. People wrote fiction before computers were invented. But I knew from experience that nothing would be achieved the old-fashioned way. Once while on a trip, I tried to use a notebook and pen, but it didn't work. Two and a half hours of agony had given rise to just three-quarters of a page covered with terrible scribbling. I tore it up angrily, realizing that it would take more time to decode it than to write it again. Once you have become accustomed to the blessings of convenience, it is hard to give them up.

As there have been no cutoffs in the meantime, the laptop primarily serves as a place where Felix can doze. I have begun to look at this as an exculpating circumstance and console myself that the investment was not completely useless after all.

Felix is otherwise an extremely clumsy tomcat. Sometimes he staggers like a drunk when he walks; when he's had enough of running he usually stops by colliding with something hard; he gets stuck in various nooks and can't get out. Once his clumsiness almost cost him his life. While still a kitten, he tried to catch a bird and only survived the fall from the third-story window because he landed in a bush.

Whenever Felix jumps onto my desk, danger threatens. Unable to stop himself on the smooth wooden surface, he slides to the first obstacle. That is usually the keyboard, monitor or printer, resulting in no damage except a bit of bruising. But I guess he's used to that by now. When there is something on the desk that can be knocked over and spilled as he slides, that's when there is real trouble.

I've stopped counting the times I have replaced the mouse or keyboard after they were ruined by coffee or tea from the cup Felix ran into. If I am on the verge of scolding him, the expression on his face always disarms me. All you can do is smile at the singular mixture of stupefaction and remorse. In addition, I too am to blame. Felix always jumps on the desk from the same side. If I kept the cup on the other side, nothing would happen. It is only right to pay the price for my mistake.

Not expecting that Felix would wake up, I had placed my tea on the left-hand side again. Only my split-second reflex spared me from disaster. Out of the corner of my eye I caught sight of calico fur silently materializing above the edge of the desk and was able to snatch the cup out of the way a moment before he jumped to the very spot where it had been. Several drops spilled on the desk, but that was nothing compared to the calamity that would have resulted from a direct hit.

Smiling, I stroked the flustered cat and then, just in case, took the cup with me into the kitchen to get a napkin to wipe up the drops of tea. I also kept the cup with me when I went back to the kitchen to throw away the wet paper. I only put it down when I reseated myself. Felix came up to sniff it, then shook his head from the lemony smell that didn't agree with him and headed for the laptop.

I sighed again as I thought how Felix's interference had once more proved fortuitous. The anger that had filled me after reading Admirer's last message had subsided in the meantime. I rarely have such feelings and they never last long. Had I answered him immediately, however, I might have said something that I would have regretted later. This way, even though I was fully entitled to be irritated by his proposal, my answer would be courteous.

Esteemed Admirer,
(This "Esteemed" would certainly have been left out
of my angry version.)

*Where did you come up with something like this? And
even if I wanted to, how could I turn over the authorship
rights to a novel?*

Sincerely,
(I would have skipped this too for sure.)
Writer

I expected a swift reply, but still jumped at the
gong that soon burst forth. Sometimes I really don't
understand myself. Why not choose a less explosive
sound? Lots of more pleasant possibilities are available.
A warbling canary, for example, or a gurgling stream.
These explosions might give me a stroke one day. Even
though cats are afraid of noise, Felix handles the gong
better than I do. He only turned his right ear slightly
towards the speakers, as though a fly had buzzed by
there, then continued to lick himself sleepily next to
the open laptop.

Highly Esteemed Writer,

*In purely technical terms, it is a simple thing to do. We
would sign a contract where everything would be set out
in detail. This sets by no means a legal precedent. You
would agree to write a novel whose authorship you would
renounce and turn over to me. I would be the sole author
of the work with full rights.*
*How I came up with this is considerably more complex.
Although at first glance my proposal might seem dishon-
est to you, please do not jump to conclusions about me. I
would like you to believe that deciding on such a step was
by no means easy. If you have ever been burdened by a*

serious decision you had to make, then you can imagine what I went through.

In one respect, however, there was no dilemma. From the outset I knew that if I ever went ahead with this, you were the only one I would approach. I am not interested in other writers. For me, your fiction has no equal. It is unique.

Sincerely,
Admirer

Someone less vain would not allow themselves to be misled by the last paragraph, but who has ever heard of a writer whose ego is not gratified by flattery, even if it is hypocritical, and particularly if it is sincere, as it seemed to be in this case. I took a sip of lukewarm tea, stroked Felix, who paid no attention and continued licking himself, then started to type.

Esteemed Admirer,

I am honored by your high opinion of my fiction. But isn't what you call its "uniqueness" the primary obstacle to your plan? Imagine for a moment—not even as the faintest hint of my consent but rather as a theoretical possibility—that I accept your proposal and write a novel that would be published under your name. Wouldn't the real writer be obvious regardless of the name on the cover? Authorship is determined more by how one writes than one's name. It is like a fingerprint and there are no two identical fingerprints. It would be easy to see who is behind the novel.

What did you mean when you wrote that "this sets by no means a legal precedent"? Are you saying that such contracts have already been concluded?

Sincerely,
Writer

Felix gave a raspy meow. Someone not in the know might easily imagine that the tomcat was not well. That's what I thought at first too. I almost took him to the vet's for a checkup. Such a weak and mournful human voice would only result if someone had a bad cold, for example, or a stomach ache. Luckily, there was nothing wrong with Felix. He simply had that kind of voice, just as his purring was barely audible.

He does not speak up very often. Usually I hear him after he has finally lost patience in front of the closed door, waiting at length for me to take notice and let him out onto the terrace. Or like now when he was signaling that he had finished washing and would like to continue his morning nap. I quickly closed the laptop and he yawned, stretched, and settled as though on a pillow. Felix otherwise likes to sleep on soft things. I don't know why he is attracted to a hard laptop. He would certainly be much more comfortable on the two-seater. But who can fathom feline fancies? I gave up long ago.

Since I have been troubled by insomnia for quite some time, I envy the speed with which he falls asleep: almost as soon as he closes his eyes. Actually, he keeps them half-closed. It gave me the creeps until I got used to it. He seems to be looking at me from another world, particularly when the twitching around his mouth indicates that he is dreaming.

Not even the new gong was able to disturb his deep sleep. I jumped again, while Felix just wiggled his right mustache. As I reached for the mouse, I wondered at Admirer's rapidity. The questions from my previous email required a certain elaboration. How could he have answered them so quickly? Less than a minute had passed since I sent my message. But this time instead of him it was one of the friends I regularly correspond with. OpenSea.

There is one bad thing about electronic mail. It

forces people to change their identity. It all starts with choosing an email address. It seems only natural for it to contain your name, but it often turns out that someone else has beaten you to it. This is no big deal for mere mortals. They aren't that particular about their name and it doesn't really matter what is in their email heading. Furthermore, it's as though they can hardly wait to be someone else.

But a writer's name is his trademark. It is inadvisable to say about a writer that he has made a name for himself, since no other kind of writer exists. If someone else has the same name, it goes without saying that the writer first comes to mind when that name is mentioned. It is therefore no wonder that writers are extremely irritated when it turns out that some anonymous person with the same name has adopted their trademark in the digital world. They consider that to be blatant theft. They would love to sue the thief, if they only knew who he was and where to file charges.

So when they find themselves in a fix and their own name is unavailable for email, writers at least have exemplary imagination when choosing a pseudonym. I, however, unexpectedly had no chance to distinguish myself in this regard. I was lucky with my first provider and could use my own name for a long time. It was not until it stopped operating a little over two and a half years ago that I too had to face the problem of a pseudonym with my second provider. What first crossed my mind was inevitable. But I had absolutely no hopes that the name would be free. If my real name, which is not very ordinary, was already taken, such an ordinary one had to have been taken long ago. How many Felixes are there in the world anyway?

Undoubtedly a lot, but even so, by some miracle I was the first one at my new provider's. Felix gave me a questioning look when I found that out. I hopped off my chair, grabbed his head between my hands and kissed him on the forehead. Such outpourings of affection are not uncommon, but I don't usually disturb him with them while he's sleeping. On this occasion, however, carried away by the excitement, I couldn't bide my time until he woke up. He eyed me sleepily for a while and then finally nodded off again. He had clearly given up trying to fathom human fancies.

The excitement was soon darkened by a tinge of jealousy. Looking at Felix's sleeping face, I was struck by the unfairness of the world. How could a tomcat be more singular than a writer? But I did not let this bad feeling go any deeper. Felix, after all, is no ordinary cat. If I was ready to consider him my co-author, then I guess one could say that he is a writer too.

Changing a writer's identity is not limited to email addresses alone, where it is compulsory, but has spread to electronic correspondence in general, although there is no obligation in this regard. Nothing stops writers from signing their emails with their real name, but many prefer to use their newly acquired pseudonym. I guess they get to liking what has been forced on them. There are certainly exceptions to this rule, but all the writers I correspond with by email present themselves as someone else. Following this line of thinking, they address me solely as Felix. This does not bother me and I reply in kind. I call them by their pseudonyms and sign as Felix. In the virtual world of writers, no one is who they really are.

Of all the pseudonyms, I found OpenSea's the least enigmatic. That was the title of his latest novel. This "latest" could also be literally his last. Almost two years have passed since it was published and there has not been even a hint of a new book. He is not the kind of writer who writes in secret. If he were writing again, perhaps not everyone would know, but I would certainly not be lacking this privileged information. That is what happened with all four of his novels. He submitted detailed reports to me on their progress during his frequent unannounced visits that would last for hours and then, when the visits stopped, in equally long phone calls at night when all I wanted was to go to bed.

He bitterly gave up on the visits when I brought Felix home. As a child he had had a traumatic encounter with a dog. I never heard the details, but he was probably bitten. The incident seems to have marked him for life; he has an aversion to animals. He cannot even stand them on his dinner plate and eats only fish. He is proud of the fact that he has never gone to a zoo.

All the kitten had to do was jump harmlessly onto his lap and he almost fell into a fit. I barely brought him round. He never crossed my doorstep again. (That was the first time I kissed Felix on the forehead.) For a while he did not even call me on the phone, and when he started again, for months he spent the first ten minutes of the conversation lecturing me about my extremely unreasonable decision to bring an animal into my home.

Although he no longer dropped by, he was still in the vicinity. I found that out from the owner of the "Open Sea" coffee bar located on the ground floor of my building, right below my study. The low hedge around the coffee bar was what saved Felix's life when he fell out the window. OpenSea went there just about every day even though he lived in a distant part of town. He always sat at the same corner table, ordered a very sweet cappuccino, opened his notebook and wrote *Open Sea* for hours.

The coffee bar is decorated in keeping with its name. The walls are covered with nautical equipment: anchors, nets, compasses, tridents, life preservers, oars, drawings of steamboats. There is even a large sailboat in a bottle on the shelf. Future literary researchers will have the difficult task of establishing whether OpenSea became a regular customer of "Open Sea" because the surroundings were favorable to *Open Sea*, which he was working on at the time, or whether the coffee bar was what inspired him to write the novel.

To my great relief, the phone calls grew less frequent and then stopped for good after OpenSea finally bought a computer. He had resisted for some considerable time, saying that not a single writer he admired had used that gadget and this had not prevented them from being giants of literary fiction, which, of course, was his own aspiration. He merely snorted derisively at my comment that the only reason they hadn't used computers was because they lived before computers were invented. That is what he always does when he runs out of arguments. After he suddenly bought a computer, I reminded him of his former aversion, but he just snorted in reply to this too.

He decided to replace the phone calls with emails when he learned of my penchant for keeping them all. His first short, rather empty messages, while he was learning to send and receive electronic mail, were soon replaced by real essays. He often checked up on whether I was duly archiving them, regretting that I had failed to immortalize our previous conversations. Once, when I asked why it was so important to him, he replied that it should actually be more important to me. If I were to publish our correspondence, that would assure me a place in literary history more than my own writing. It was no small achievement to have a role in the book *Conversations with a Giant*, even if only as the person asking the questions.

Actually, I never asked any questions and none were ever needed. OpenSea did that all by himself. His correspondence was devoted solely to analyzing his books. Almost every email started with a rhetorical question verifying my cleverness. Inspired by a new reading of his works—as though that was all he had read for quite some time—he would ask whether I could grasp all the subtlety of some special aspect of his novels. It made no difference what I replied or whether I replied at all because it was understood that I was unable to get to the heart of the matter and that I needed to be enlightened.

I first realized he was not planning on writing a fifth novel when no mention was made of it. Interpreting his first three books to me, when the tangle of meaning became apparently impenetrable, he periodically mentioned that in any case the important topics he dealt with (unimportant topics were clearly out of the question) could not be exhausted in only one work and that he was already thinking of the next novel that would complete the given topic.

I might have overlooked this missing announcement of a new book had he not drawn my attention to it himself. He repeatedly mentioned writers who had committed one of the worst sins lying in wait for men of the pen: they continued to write and publish books even when they had nothing more to say. A serious writer must know when to stop. Ideally, this would be after one's best work. And he hadn't the slightest doubt: he had reached his peak in *Open Sea*. Indeed, he had claimed the same thing for each of his previous novels, particularly for the first, but there was an extenuating circumstance for these erroneous appraisals. He had made them before writing *Open Sea*.

The short email I had just received was, as always, devoid of the formal politeness of correspondence. The message's sender and the recipient were known to one another, so there was no need to waste words. Later, when editing the book for printing, phrases such as "Dear Friend" and "Sincerely yours, Giant" could be added.

I was sure that he had started a new chapter of interpretation on his own work, but was mistaken. The question was quite unexpected.

Have you ever thought of writing under a pseudonym?

I stared for a few moments, bewildered by what was written on the screen. As far as I could remember, we had never talked about pseudonyms.

No, I haven't. Why?

I wrote this under the question and sent him the email. It irritates him when I keep the text of his message. I once tried to find out why, but he just replied angrily that it was self-evident. It did not seem like that to me, so I continued doing things my way. I might have stopped if it didn't get on his nerves.

I drank up my tea and headed for the kitchen. As I was washing the cup in the sink, two gongs came one after the other from my study. If this continues, I thought, I won't get any writing done today. Frustration and relief started jockeying for position inside me.

OpenSea had already replied.

There are advantages to a pseudonym.

What is he up to, I wondered as I saved the new message. I pondered over what to do next. Not sending an immediate reply was an option, particularly since he had not asked any questions this time. That would raise his blood pressure even more: another thing he considers self-evident is that I have an obligation to answer him immediately, whereas, naturally, this does not apply to him. But I was curious to find out where this thing about pseudonyms was heading.

What, for example?

I had mistakenly assumed that the other email was from Admirer. It seems I had asked him a difficult question and he needed more time to answer. This one was from Banana.

Of course. I had forgotten what day it was. For almost a year and a half, every Wednesday morning she has regularly reported what she dreamed the night before. Dreams visit her on other nights of the week as well, but she considers them to have no literary value. Only the dreams she has when she goes to sleep on a Tuesday night count. She has never told me why. Banana generally explains very little.

Once I asked her if she liked bananas. It was a polite way to find out why she had chosen that pseudonym for electronic correspondence. She replied that she was not fond of fruit. She used it primarily for cosmetic purposes. Kiwi and pineapple in particular. She didn't elaborate. If she caught onto why I had inquired, she did nothing to show it.

I have only met Banana once. She sat next to me in a half-empty hall during a literary evening. I stared in disbelief at her extremely large figure as she came up to me. It looked like an extravagantly decorated ocean liner was gliding my way. Her pink parasol-like hat pranced with a bouquet of colorful feathers. Judging by the size, they must have come from an enormous bird. If I had worn even half as many chains around my neck, my head would be constantly bowed. Some were silver and gold, but most were copper and stone costume jewelry. There was no way of telling where one piece of clothing ended and another began. I was not even sure what some of them were called. If I were to dress so gaudily, I could easily pass for a harlequin. The dark-brown purse she carried was proportionate to her size: it was bigger than a mailman's satchel. Finally, I would not have been able to walk in the bright red spike-heeled shoes and probably could not even have stood up in them.

But her round face outdid everything else. Only

someone wanting to disguise themselves would have put on so much makeup. Her forehead looked like a freshly baked cake sprinkled with silver powdered sugar. Her pale blue eye shadow extended halfway to her ears. Her cheeks were as red as if someone had just pinched them. Her wild chestnut lipstick almost doubled the size of her lips. The rest of her skin was covered with a layer of pancake makeup as thick as butter spread on Melba toast. The thought of kissing this woman disgusted me.

When the chair next to me started to creak underneath her, I decided to throw politeness to the wind and move several seats away. We simply did not go together. I felt inquisitive and malicious eyes turning towards us from all around. But Banana spared me any embarrassment. The right word at the right time has amazing power.

"I finished reading your first book yesterday," she said softly, barely moving her lips, as though confiding something to me. "It's excellent."

I might still have thought twice about kissing her, but the makeup and general appearance suddenly seemed less garish. In any case, I no longer saw any reason to change seats so rudely. We started talking in whispers, like conspirators or lovers, even though there was no one close to us. When we stopped, the literary evening was already well underway.

The first thing she told me was that I appeared more enigmatic in person than in my jacket photograph. I looked at her questioningly. More enigmatic? Yes, she repeated, but instead of explaining she added that she had bought the rest of my books too. She was getting ready to read them one after the other. What order did I suggest? I thought it over. Chronological. (She had caught me off guard with the question. No other way came to mind.) Would I like to hear what she thought after each book? Of course, I would be delighted. She would prefer to send it in writing. Did I have an email address? By all means. I quickly handed her my business card.

Her first impressions arrived only three days later. I have an aversion to speed readers. I find it disrespectful when someone rushes through a book that took me months to write. The bulk of my effort would go unnoticed in a superficial reading. With Banana, however, speed was not to the detriment of perception. She had a talent for noting subtleties. Some had even escaped me.

Since she only had words of praise, I started waiting impatiently for each subsequent book report. A sense of dread filled me when she failed to write for a full nine days after her impressions about my fourth book. Indeed, the fifth was more voluminous, but I had calculated that she could finish it in four and a half days, reading at her previous tempo. Something might have hampered her. But how could I expect her to put everything else on hold in order to keep company with my books? I knew nothing about her, nothing about her obligations, which she certainly must have had. There is no ideal reader who has nothing else to do but read your books.

What if she did not like the book and was reluctant to tell me? It was an awkward thing to ask straight out in an email, but if we were to meet somewhere, I might be able to find out indirectly. Conversations in the flesh have advantages. You learn things not only from the words but from facial expressions as well. Even when concealed by too much makeup.

I invited her to join me at another literary evening. She replied that she would love to come, but did not appear. An email was waiting for me at home. She was sorry she hadn't come. She hadn't had time to get ready. If only I had invited her earlier and not just five and a half hours beforehand. The rest of the message cheered me up. She was delighted with my fifth book. She hadn't written earlier because she had read it twice.

I proposed that we attend two more literary evenings. The first invitation came one day in advance and for the other I gave her three full days' notice. Even this was not enough. I felt like asking her how long it had taken to get ready the only time we had met, but how could I insult someone with such a high opinion of my writing? We never saw each other again, but luckily there were the emails.

She read all of my books in thirty-seven days. I took this as a compliment, but not without a tinge of bitterness. The short time it took her to read them was greatly disproportionate to the more than eleven years it had taken me to write them. But who is to blame for my slow writing? Would I have preferred it to take her just as long to read them? In any case, the discrepancy was only apparent. If all the time people spent reading my books were added together, it would probably balance out a decade of writing. The total reading time might even have an edge, despite the fact that I am not considered a widely read writer.

Even before I received the last report, I realized what a pity it would be for me to be the only one to read Banana's impressions of my books. They were more insightful and to the point than many reviews. To say nothing of the fact that they were extremely laudatory. After she had read my entire opus, I proposed that we publish her texts somewhere. I was quite willing to help her with this and even suggested that with a little more work, they might become a book.

She replied that she was flattered by my proposal, but unfortunately could not accept. She would rather not appear in print as a literary critic because she saw herself solely as a writer. This surprised me. There hadn't been even a hint in her previous emails that she too was a writer. In reply to my amazement, she said she wasn't. At least not yet. Her first book was still in the preparation phase.

I soon learned what these preparations were all about. She confided in me reluctantly, saying she expected it to remain strictly between us. Along with all the rest, I said soothingly. Her book appeared in her dreams. Once a week, always on the night between Tuesday and Wednesday, she dreamed parts that she later wrote down.

How long had this been going on? Almost a year and a half. She had collected sixty-nine episodes. Why, that's almost a complete novel, I said. Oh, no. She was far from the end. It would take some time before she finished it. I thought of the modest length of most of my books. A certain discomfort filled me even though I knew, of course, that a book's value is not judged by its thickness.

What was the novel about? Banana's answer seemed to start with a sigh. If only she could tell me. Everything was still very fragmented. The episodes did not form any whole. It was like having the parts of a puzzle before her without any idea what the puzzle looked like. I would see for myself. She sent me an email with sixty-nine attachments denoted only by numbers. It also contained a short and gratuitous message in red letters: "For your eyes only." Since she had been very diligent in reading my books, I had to respond in kind. I spent the next day and a half with her dreams.

There was no reason to fear that the pieces awaiting me would be like most of those I receive for assessment from beginners: confused and illiterate. Based on Banana's impressions about my works, I knew that she was quite skilled at writing coherently and also knew how to spell. Nevertheless, being a successful essayist is no guarantee that fiction will come easily. Yet she got along just fine. She had a particular sense for metaphors. I experienced several pangs of envy.

She was right about the loose-knit structure. The episodes were so diverse that they did not seem to belong to the same puzzle. It was not at all apparent how they could fit together into a whole. I broke this to her gently, first showering praise on the virtues of her debut. She replied with surprising cheerfulness. The lack of a whole did not worry her very much. It was only temporary. Everything would fit together in the end. A dream would come along that would miraculously connect all the others.

I do not believe in miracles in writing fiction, but there was no reason to trouble Banana's self-confidence with my doubts. I replied that I would find this pivotal dream very interesting. This gave her a chance to ask whether I would like to receive the new episodes after she wrote them down each Wednesday. I could not refuse, of course.

Although Banana did not openly ask it of me, somehow it went without saying that I would write up my comments on each new piece. Not just a sentence or two: I had to make an effort or else I would fall short of her extensive impressions of my work. It went smoothly at first, but as the weeks followed with no end in sight, I found it harder and harder. I cursed my vanity for making me so recklessly beholden. Who could tell how long it would take to repay the debt. Wednesday became the most hated day of the week.

I naïvely hoped that it all might end with the hundredth dream, but Banana disregarded round numbers and the following episodes were more diverse than ever. It was increasingly apparent that there was no pivotal dream nor could there ever be one. We had already reached the one hundred thirty-sixth part and she showed no sign of tiring, but my strength was giving out. I had to do something, even if it meant losing an admirer.

Now as I looked at her regular Wednesday message, I thought that this might be the time to put an end to this story that clearly had no end. Very politely, but firmly. Besides, what could she hold against me? I had duly repaid her in kind. The volume of what I had written in sixty-nine short texts on her dreams was approximately the same as her impressions about my books. Had I done my own writing instead, I would have another book by now. Shorter than the others, indeed, but a book nonetheless.

When I opened Banana's email and saw the red letters, I knew this was something out of the ordinary. The message consisted of just two words: Pivotal dream. I squinted fixedly at the words for a few moments and then hastened to open the attached file entitled "137". I expected the longest text to date. Considering everything that had to be connected and explained, I would not have been surprised if it were as long as the total of everything that had preceded it. But the file contained just one paragraph.

In my dream I find you in my study. You are sitting at my computer. I go up to you, bewildered. Even though you can hear me, you do not turn around. I look over your shoulder. "Pivotal Dream" is written at the top of the screen and the rest is filled with dense writing. You are typing quickly, as though playing an upbeat composition on a piano. I want to ask you something, but you raise your finger briefly to your lips without turning around and signal me to be quiet. I settle into a nearby armchair. I am filled with joy as I watch you write as though spellbound. I could never have finished it without you. The tapping sound of the keyboard is more and more like music. The beat picks up. You gesticulate like a real musician. The ecstasy is transferred to me. I feel like I'm on fire. The crescendo approaches. I stand up. At the high point you jump from the chair, open your arms and finally turn towards me. Two radiant faces gaze at each other in silence, and then you say breathlessly: "Finished!"

What was this supposed to mean? How could it be the pivotal dream? It didn't resolve anything. Now everything was woollier than ever before. And what was I doing in her dream? Fair enough, you can't choose who you dream about. Once I dreamed about her too, not long after our one and only meeting. Probably because her garish appearance was still fresh in my mind. But it had only been an ordinary dream. This was literature.

Was she trying to tell me something in a roundabout way? All right, she was not inclined to go into detail, but we still had to get things clear. We could not leave it like this. Particularly now that I was more deeply involved than I liked.

I had just reopened the window with her email to reply, when two gongs came one after the other again. What a difference from yesterday, I thought gloomily, when I received four messages in total, two of them spam. And today there seemed to be no end to them and not a single one was spam. Yesterday I had wanted more and now I was bothered by their large number. One is hard to please.

Usually I would look at the new emails first, but now Banana took precedence.

Dear Banana,

What an exciting dream, no doubt about it. I am honored to be a part of it, although it clearly must be my far superior double. First of all, there is no way I could be the pianist at the keyboard because I use only my right index finger when I type. And who has ever achieved ecstasy with one finger? But my double surpasses me far more in another way. Hats off to his brilliance in writing the key chapter. My poor talent would never do the trick. I will wait impatiently until next Wednesday in hopes that I finally get a chance to read it.

Humbly yours,
Felix

Admirer's email was not in my inbox this time either. OpenSea had sent the first and P-0 the second. Had he changed his mind and given up? Too bad. I was really interested to see how he would reply.

What advantages?—OpenSea asked in return. *Isn't it obvious? First of all, you can use a pseudonym to publish things you wouldn't want to come out under your own name.*

I still could not figure out his intentions, but there had to be something behind this. He hadn't started this business about pseudonyms just to pass the time. I would have to be on my guard.

I do want everything I write to come out in my name. I have no need for a pseudonym.

This time I did not keep the text from his email.

The message from P-0 was atypical. It had no attachment, unlike the eighty-seven previous ones that each contained a pastiche.

Even though I have been corresponding with P-0 for nineteen months, I know little else about him except that he lives somewhere far away. I have no idea what he looks like. Indeed, this is not unusual. At least half the people I am in internet contact with are faceless to me. Sometimes I imagine what they look like based on what they say, but that is not a very reliable guide.

Once we got to know each other better, I thought of asking P-0 to send me a photo. But I was afraid of putting him on the spot. What if he had some reason not to? Not everyone is happy with their looks. I damped down my curiosity and did not even ask for his real name. If he had wanted me to know, he would have told me.

On the other hand, I was not faceless to him. He knew my name, of course, and had seen my picture at the top of my website. That is how he had gotten in touch with me, as had most of my readers. Sometimes I get strange proposals from them, but P-0's surpassed them all.

He asked whether I would let him write pastiches based on my stories, which delighted him. He had already written one and enclosed it as an attachment. Curious, I opened the file with the short name "P-1" and found a surprise waiting in the very first line. I had assumed that he would keep P-0 as the author's pseudonym. It did not seem very likely that I would be able to discover his true identity there. The last thing I expected, however, was to see my own name.

Bewildered, I started reading. It was a variation on my first story. The plot had been changed slightly and thus the sequence of events, and particularly the dénouement. Some characters had disappeared and others had appeared. Two episodes were added. Everything was tight-knit and consistent, even imaginative. I would not have minded being the author myself. Just as important was the fact that the story's tone was faithfully reproduced. The careful choice of words and expressions was a highly contributory factor in this regard. I would have used the same ones. An exemplary pastiche in all respects. P-0 was not a mere beginner.

The experience was extremely unusual: reading my story that was not mine. The story was similar enough to mine that it really could have been mine and yet it was different, but not so different that it could not be mine. Where it was similar, it seemed as though I had written it, and where it was different, it was as though I could have written it. If you didn't know which came first, you could even have thought that my story was a pastiche—and the pastiche the original story.

I gave him the permission he sought. I did it not just because P-0 was free to write whatever he wanted without my permission, even pastiches of my stories. (How could I stop him?) Nor even primarily because I was flattered that someone was doing it. (How many writers live to see their stories used for a pastiche?) What counted was the realization that I was not losing anything with these pastiches. Quite the contrary, one might say. Even though they were not my stories, it was just as though they were. As though I had written something I hadn't. I had no qualms about this. I had not appropriated something that belonged to someone else. It was not I who had put my name at the beginning which, in any case, was the other author's pseudonym.

Nevertheless, one condition went along with my permission: P-0 was not allowed to publish any of it. This was to avoid any confusion that would arise if my stories that really were mine came out at the same time as my stories that were not mine, and were signed with my name. In addition, what if the readers, or even worse the critics, decided that they preferred the pastiches to the original stories? Even though I did not mention this latter reason to P-0, of course, he readily accepted my condition. He had never intended to publish them.

The pastiches arrived at uneven intervals, sometimes as many as three a week, while sometimes there would be three weeks between them. He kept to the original order in which the stories had been written. I soon began to await each new pastiche eagerly. The excitement that rekindled inside me almost resembled that I had felt when writing the original works.

Even though I knew there was something wrong about it, the growth of my parallel opus of sorts filled me with pride. Since it never failed to please me, I began to think what a shame it was that no one but the two of us would ever know about it. Was there still a chance for it to see the light of day? I told P-0 that I might be willing to change my attitude about publishing it, but he turned out to be more steadfast than I. He did not want the pastiches to come out.

This exasperated me. He wasn't the only one involved. True enough, P-0 was the formal author, but these stories were basically mine. Not to mention that they were signed with my name, even as someone's pseudonym. I should have thought that I had the right to be heard too. Why are you writing them if you don't want to publish anything, I asked him angrily. For the sake of practice, he replied. He would start to publish his own work when he became skilled enough at writing pastiches of my stories. He would like to continue collaborating when that time came too.

I did not exactly regard what we were doing as collaboration. Well, maybe it could be called that, broadly speaking. I expected him to explain what he had specifically in mind, but he never mentioned the subject again and I felt it was not my place to ask. There was actually no need. Only a few of my stories remained. Soon, when he had written pastiches of them all, we would see what form this continued collaboration took.

The last, eighty-seventh pastiche had arrived just under three weeks ago. I had thought that he would get in touch earlier, but he had fallen completely silent. I wondered at one point what to do if he broke off contact with me. I could not publish the pastiches without P-0's permission. They were as much his as mine. If not more so. It was hard to weigh it exactly.

But here he was again, thank heavens. And on this tumultuous day. Let's hear what he had in mind.

Dear Felix,
(At first he had addressed me by my real name preceded with "Esteemed Mr." but since it seemed incongruous for me to be real and for him to be P-0, I soon

proposed that we shift to Felix. Besides, that is how I had signed our correspondence from the beginning, out of inertia. He readily accepted this change as a sign of increased familiarity between us.)

First, I owe you an immeasurable debt of gratitude. Had it not been for your kind consent to let me acquire experience writing pastiches of your stories, and for the patience and goodwill with which you read them, I would never have mustered the courage to take my chances as a writer. But just when it seemed that the time had finally come for me to strike out on my own, something that I had been sensing for some time proved true. Standing on my own writing legs will not be so easy. The long time I spent with your stories has had a deeper impact on me than I expected. You, of course, are not in the slightest to blame for that, but your shadow hovers over everything I have tried to write by myself. Regardless of what I write, it still seems like a pastiche. I was terribly disturbed at first, but then it dawned on me: why not turn this difficulty to my advantage? Instead of avoiding it, I will embrace it. I will simply continue writing pastiches of your stories. With your esteemed permission, of course.

Sincerely yours,
P-0

I reread the email to make sure I had not missed anything and then sighed. Just as I started my reply, the gong announced a new message. Had I been writing a longer letter, I would have interrupted my writing for a moment to see who it was from, but everything I had to say to P-0 could fit into one and a half sentences.

Dear P-0,

I'm afraid I don't quite understand: how can you con-

*tinue to write pastiches of my stories when you have al-
ready written one for each of them?*

 Sincerely yours,
 Felix

I sent the email and then moved the cursor towards
my virtual mailbox, but it did not get there because Felix opened his eyes just then and let out a sharp meow.

The first time that happened, soon after I brought
him home, my blood had run cold. The kitten had
seemed to be sleeping peacefully and then suddenly started mewing in distress. I wasn't sure what had
caused it, so I didn't know what to do. There had been
no sudden sound or anything else disrupting the customary peace in my study. It was not until the fourth
sudden awakening that I understood what was going
on. The disturbance had come from inside, not outside.
Felix had been frightened by a dream.

He reacted like a baby and burst into tears. And just
like a baby, he had to be soothed. He would usually
go back to sleep after a brief scratch behind the ears, a
stroking of his back and some calming words. It rarely
happened that a bad dream woke him up completely.
Then I would have to pet him at length until I got the
agitation to leave his eyes.

That's how it was now. As I stroked him patiently,
first he looked at me with eyes as big as saucers, as
though still seeing the monster from his dream. His
eyes softened slowly, but he did not close them again.
He got up languidly and stretched, arching his back,
yawned widely and then got off the laptop, wobbling
slightly. He stood hesitantly on the edge of my desk a
few moments and jumped. He landed awkwardly at
the best of times and even more so when he was groggy.

I did not have to watch him to know where he was
headed. When he woke up, he usually waddled to-

wards the plastic kitty box in the bathroom. Soon I would have to replace the old newspapers that cover the bottom of the box and pour a little sand over them from the bag under the bathroom sink. Since Felix takes his time with such matters, I had time to open the new email.

You are wrong, as usual—wrote OpenSea. *Only an utterly self-centered writer would want everything he writes to come out in his own name.*

There was only one way to reply to this. Once again I kept the text of his message.

As far as I know, you have yet to use a pseudonym.

As I saved the last two emails, I could hear Felix scratching at the sand-covered paper. When I got there, he had already left the box and headed for the kitchen. Just as I started to pick up the wet newspaper, the first gong sounded. I heard the second one, more muffled, from the terrace as I put the newspaper in the dark-gray garbage bag.

I did not go straight back to my study, but headed after Felix to give him his breakfast. He was standing with his tail raised next to the pink double food and water bowl. I opened a new green bag of cat food and poured out about one third. He spent a few moments sniffing it inquisitively before starting to eat.

When he was still a kitten, he was able to devour almost a full bag at every meal. I watched in disbelief as he voraciously gulped it down, wondering where he put it all. His little stomach was the most conspicuous part of his body. As he grew, he toned down and his figure became better proportioned. For quite some time, one bag has been enough to last him the whole day. He eats less now but is very choosy. I must bear his likes and dislikes carefully in mind. How many times has he just sniffed at what I put out and walked indifferently away? When that happens, I feel like not giving him anything else until he finishes it, but soon renege, throw out the food he doesn't like and open a new bag.

Felix has trouble chewing because he broke an incisor, so I have to purée everything that is the slightest bit hard. Crackers are the only exception and he loves them, even if it is an effort to crumble them in his mouth. The vet proposed putting a cap on the broken tooth, but I said no because it could only be done under anesthesia. When he came out of the anesthesia after he was fixed, it was so traumatic for both of us that I simply could not go through it again. So what if he makes a mess when he eats, we are both used to it.

I returned to my desk and looked at my virtual mailbox. The first email was from Banana and the second was from Pandora. I saved them and then opened Banana's.

Dear Felix,

I admire your humility, but this was no double. I might be fooled in a waking state, but not in a dream. I know perfectly well that it was you, just as I know that you are the only one capable of writing the key chapter. I suspected this as soon as I started reading your first book, and when I saw you, I knew for sure. That is why I went to that literary evening. It was not a chance meeting. I had hoped you would turn up. I was told that you often attend literary gatherings.

You must help me finish my first novel. I won't be able to do it by myself. You will have nothing to read next Wednesday. There will be no more literary dreams.

You must not underestimate the power of one finger. A real virtuoso needs nothing more. How many times have you thrilled me with what you did with only your right index finger?

In any case, I did not tell you my whole dream last time. After you finished playing, you jumped up from the chair and turned towards me. What a sight! You only had clothes from behind, while you were completely naked in front. . . .

Yours alone,
Banana

I shook my head. This was what a man deserved when he was not only vain but naïve. It had all been planned from the start. Even so, she underestimated me. Did she really think I would keep on playing the fool easily duped by flattery, that I would be concerned about her future as a writer or that she could induce me to write the pivotal chapter with this half-nakedness? In any case, nothing would have worked, not even a much better lure. Even if I wanted to, I was unable to write what she needed. I doubt whether anyone could.

Dear Banana,

Now it is quite certain that you did not dream about me. I would not be so kinkily half-dressed or half-bare even in a dream.

Sincerely,
Felix

I do not know why Pandora chose such a nickname in the digital world, but I doubt she would have kept her real name even if she could. Anyone with a name like that undoubtedly feels awkward with themselves and can hardly wait to change it.

I knew Pandora by sight for more than four years

before we officially met. We live in the same building, I am on the third floor and she is on the top, sixth floor. We would meet periodically at the entrance or in front of the elevator, but there would only be a nod of the head, a smile and an occasional word.

She is a short, stout woman on the threshold of 70, with gray but still luxuriant hair, and is always elegantly dressed, even when she is just going to the local grocery store. Her oversized glasses with thick lenses have a little chain to keep them around her neck. She used to teach piano at a music school. When she retired, she gave private lessons for a while and then stopped for some reason.

We spoke for the first time in the waiting room at the vet's. I had brought Felix to be fixed and she had brought Albert for chronic constipation. Albert is a rather old German shepherd that has trouble walking and drools all the time. He has watery eyes and scruffy hair. He is very good-natured. He didn't get his hackles up then because Felix was around. Felix stayed unruffled too.

She must have guessed by the look on my face why we had come to the vet's. I had spent a sleepless night and she tried to console me. Yes, you are about to do a terrible thing, but it is inevitable when you keep a cat in an apartment. She'd had a tomcat named Leopold before Albert. Even though it happened long ago, she could still remember how much she suffered over his castration. It had actually been easier on Leopold than on her. After he recovered from the operation, he continued his carefree life. He was not even aware of what he had lost, so it had not been hard on him. He lived to a ripe old age in blessed ignorance.

Seeing that she had not cheered me up very much, she added, a little shyly, that she enjoyed my books. She had thought of telling me earlier during one of our chance meetings, but held back, not wanting to appear intrusive. She cited the books that she had especially liked. (They were all wonderful, of course, but these were exceptional.) My face brightened, as expected. I even smiled briefly.

That is when I found out that Pandora also wrote. For years. With no intention of publishing anything. For her own pleasure. She would never think of proposing that I read any of it, she could just imagine how many requests of this type I received from beginners. (I sighed at this, raising my eyebrows.) But if I did find a little time, I might be intrigued. I appeared as the protagonist in some of her stories. Of course I found the time.

She sent me her stories by email even though I proposed that she drop by for a cup of coffee or tea and give me a printed copy. She thanked me for the invitation, she would love to come, but unfortunately she could not leave her apartment for long. She only went out when there was no way of avoiding it. She had to be with Albert all the time. He was almost totally blind and his hearing was very bad. She did not dare leave him alone for very long. He became confused as soon as he felt she was gone and that certainly was not good for his weak heart. And his other organs were failing too. Now he was having trouble with constipation. He had not produced a thing in three days. What's to be done; old age. We all have that in store for us.

I had hoped that she would invite me to visit her, but she asked for my email address instead. We started corresponding on almost a daily basis from a distance of three floors. She sent me her stories, but we mostly spoke at length about Felix, Albert and Leopold. She knew what it was to live with a cat and gave me lots of useful advice. Our meetings in the hallways, however, continued to be brief. Someone not in the know would conclude that we barely knew each other. Nothing indicated that we had become close virtual friends.

Pandora's stories were actually sketches: highly sentimental descriptions of small events, almost always with animals. Snails crawling in all directions on the park paths after rain. A shop window full of birds whose joyful song was muffled. A squirrel crawling along a bent linden branch and landing on a windowsill. A flock of bats squeakily scouting the evening sky. Butterflies quivering on top of wildflowers. A kitten dizzy from chasing its own tail. A mouse that chewed through an old book.

She used too many adjectives but otherwise had a polished way with a sentence and a certain talent for the picturesque. One would say that she was rather well-read. If I had the chance to visit her, I would probably find a large book collection. I could just imagine the books I would find. Literature for Pandora was the idealized refuge of the lonely. Just like music.

It was quite odd to come across myself as the hero of a story. Hero is too strong a word, though, because, except for me, there were no other characters, at least not human ones. I was really nothing but a bit player. I followed the snails as they meandered down the path, strained my ears to hear the soundless birdsong in the store, stood stock still so as not to disturb the squirrel at the window, watched in wonder and awe as the bats circled above my head, reached for the swarm of butterflies with cupped hands, laughed at the whirling kitten and gazed benevolently as the mouse damaged the thick volume.

How did I even know it was me since I had no name and was never described? Most of all because I was carrying one of my books in each story. Indeed this was not a special sign, it could have been in the hands of someone else, but Pandora did not fail to mention deftly that the writer never parted from his books.

Periodically I was tempted to suggest that she flesh out my character. I felt confined in the role she had assigned me. But I feared that this would be asking too much of her. Had she wanted and been able to write differently, she would have done so. I had to be satisfied with the humble place I had in literature. As a hero, that is.

Pandora had introduced two changes in her more recent stories. First, I stopped being nameless. I became Felix, which removed any doubt that it was me. In addition, the previous assortment of animals narrowed down completely.

Besides me there was only Albert. In most cases, various things would happen to us while I was taking him for a walk. For no apparent reason he would bark at an oak tree where he had just urinated, run after dry leaves blowing in the wind on the tree-lined paths, try to dig up a molehill, shake off clouds of drops after entering a small fishpond, roll in the sandbox at an empty playground.

I suspected that these were actually Pandora's adventures with Albert from his younger days. I could only guess why she had ceded this role to me. Was this a roundabout way of letting me know that she was unable to take the dog for a walk and that my help would be welcomed? I offered to take her place, but the problem turned out to be with Albert and not with her. He no longer had the strength to go out, even briefly, although it would do him good. All he had left were these fictional walks with me, which Pandora assured me he enjoyed quite well. I shook my head at this, but nevertheless the role I had in her stories suddenly did not seem so modest.

I was certain that she was now sending me a new story with Albert, but I was mistaken.

Dear Mr. Felix,
(Although she signed herself as Pandora from the outset, for a long time she avoided addressing me by

my nickname. She said she found it hard to deprive a well-known writer of his well-known name. As I continued to be Felix in my correspondence with her, for a while she only put "Dear Sir". She did not accept my nickname until I was given a name in her sketches— after I started taking Albert for his virtual walks.)

Unfortunately, I have sad news about Albert. It seems his end is nigh. The vet just came to see him after a very difficult night. All he could do was give him something to ease the pain. He doubted he would make it through the next night.

Even though I knew it was approaching, now that the moment is almost here I realize that I am not at all prepared. Who is ever prepared for the death of someone close? And I have no one dearer than Albert. When he goes, I will be utterly alone.

That is, unless you help me with the kindness of your heart. I realize that what I humbly ask is quite unfitting, but the gulf of despair yawning before me forces me to take no heed of the scruples that I have held all my life.

I read Albert the stories where you and he are together. I know how foolish that must seem to you, but they truly make him feel a little bit better, offering him solace. Perhaps literature could now give me the same solace, regardless of how foolish.

I have dared to think that you might be so kind as to consent to write a novel about Albert. I would read it every day, thereby creating the illusion that he is still with me. I am convinced that this will make my solitude easier to bear.

Surely you would ask, why not do it myself since I've already written stories about Albert. Two reasons stand in the way. When Albert is no more, I will not be able to write a single word about him. And even if I could, my unskilled writing would only dishonor his memory. He deserves nothing but the pen of the best master of fiction.

And that is you in all respects. In addition, you are the only writer to know him in both the realities in which we are given to exist.

I remain humbly hopeful that you will have mercy on a poor old woman.

With my deepest admiration,
Pandora

What was happening today? It was as though they had all conspired to ask impossible services from me. All right, not all of them, OpenSea was an exception, but he was being rather strange too. The way things were going, he just might join the others soon, and he would be capable of thinking up something really twisted. If this weren't happening to me in reality and I was reading about it in some book instead, I would criticize the writer for going too far. Even two such requests in the same day would be unconvincing, let alone five, which is how many there could be in the end. But reality does not stick to the rules of fiction.

So what should I do now? I certainly couldn't refuse Pandora as easily as I had Banana. Hers was not a twisted entreaty but a desperate cry for help. But did she realize what she was asking of me? A novel, no less. As though a novel can be written just like that, just like a sketch, and on order to boot. All right, maybe some writers can do that but I am certainly not one of them. Even if I agreed, it would not be at all certain that I would be capable of writing anything about Albert, even a story. I am not a general practitioner who takes on whatever topic you give him. In any case, I have never written about dogs. Not even about cats, although they are much closer to me.

Nevertheless, I must be very tactful with Pandora: not agree to what she asked but in such a way that it did not seem like a refusal. Under no circumstances should she get the impression that I had turned my back on her at this difficult moment, or that I had made her a promise that later I would not be able keep. I brought the cursor to the reply mail icon, but did not click on it. I stayed there a few moments, lost in thought, searching for the right words.

Dear Mrs. Pandora,
(She was actually Miss, but "Mrs." seemed more suitable at the outset and never once did she correct me.)

I was shaken by your news of Albert's serious state. Is there truly nothing that can be done? Have you thought of consulting another specialist? Miracles are taking place today in veterinary science and medicine in general. I simply refuse to believe that his end is imminent.

Should the sad prospect nonetheless come to pass, please count on my assistance in all respects. I am here to take care of all the practical matters and to be with you for as long as you like. You will certainly not be alone.

I am extremely honored at the faith you have put in my humble writing abilities. I will do my very best not to let you down. I do not know whether you will like my future story about Albert, but please believe that I will write it from the heart.

With my deepest respects,
Felix

As I typed, my speakers reverberated twice, but I did not stop. I only looked at my virtual mailbox after I had saved and sent my reply to Pandora. The first message was from OpenSea and the second was from Admirer. So he had not changed his mind after all. I was really curious about what he had to say, but order prevailed. Emails that come first have precedence.

I, of course, am something else—wrote OpenSea. *Under certain circumstances, however, even I could resort to a pseudonym.*

It always went without saying that he was something else. We had started writing at about the same time. He had duly informed me in a solemn voice that he was starting work on his first novel, convinced that this was a major-league event in contemporary literary history. What else could it be? Long preparations at the pinnacle of literature had blazed the way. For decades he had been training on the examples of great men through the classes he taught at the University. Now that he had penetrated to the very essence of this art, what would be more natural than finally to join the giants himself? Nothing less than that was good enough for him.

He sullenly received the news that I too had started to write, although I did not mention any pinnacles and giants. He asked whether I was at all aware of what I was doing. People today think that mere literacy is guarantee enough to try their hand at writing. That is the same as thinking that all you need to become a painter is art supplies. Only those who have thoroughly studied literature can ever dream of creating something.

There was no sense in responding to this. It would only lead to a pointless debate. I continued writing without telling him about it. He, on the other hand, regularly reported his progress to me. Not only did I enjoy the privilege of having him read new chapters to me, he also did me the honor of interpreting them. Periodically he would ask to see something I had written. This inevitably gave rise to his reproving advice to drop a task in which I was clearly out of my depth.

He did not give up even years later when my books had already come out in foreign languages. Indeed, some sort of explanation had to be given for this unnatural phenomenon. The opposite was to be expected—for his books to appear around the world and for no one to know about mine but my closest friends, who mostly did not read them and just kept them on the shelf.

OpenSea proved quite ingenious at interpreting this injustice. First he grumbled that the only reason I was published was because I wrote genre literature, while his, of course, was highbrow and as such one could not expect today's illiterate publishers to understand it. He sniffed in reply to my bewildered question as to what genre he had in mind.

Then he concluded that I had achieved a degree of success owing to his constant support in mentoring my writing. If my email-collecting mania had been an embarrassment to me before this, just then it filled me with pleasure. He may have forgotten our earlier conversations on the subject when he still dropped by my place, but there was a mass of later messages filled with "support" in the form of untiring efforts to discourage me from writing. I did not remind him of them, though, just as I did not ask the difficult question: how did he fail as a mentor to himself, while he succeeded with me? I knew that he would sniff at that too.

Finally, he came up with a third explanation. So many of my books were in print owing not to their literary value, of course, but to my resourcefulness. He, unfortunately, was greatly lacking in this regard. If he were only half as resourceful as I, what a success he would be. I could not quarrel with this statement. At least as far as his lack of resourcefulness was concerned.

It seems my suspicions were right. OpenSea had a surprise for me too, although it still was not clear what kind. What could have led him to contemplate a pseudonym, he who had such a high opinion of his literary name?

Really?—I replied. *Under what circumstances?*

I saved this, sent it to OpenSea and then hurried to open Admirer's email.

Highly Esteemed Writer,

Please forgive me for my belated reply. I was hindered by circumstances beyond my control.

You are right, of course. One's writing style is unique. But it can be imitated. Rest assured, this is what will first come to mind if a book appears that bears your stamp in all respects except that it is signed by another name. This would actually be a compliment for you. Is there any better confirmation of a writer's excellence than to imitate him? No one could hold anything against you. Quite the contrary, everyone would admire you. Objections could only be addressed to the imitator.

I am puzzled at your question as to whether contracts such as the one I proposed have already been concluded. It is hard for me to believe that such an experienced writer as you could be so uninformed. Why, this is an open secret. But if it really is something new to you, I suggest that you familiarize yourself with the matter. You will be amazed when you find out all the books that result from similar arrangements. . . .

Sincerely,
Admirer

I leaned my elbows on the edge of my desk and rested my chin in my interlaced fingers, just as I do when playing chess with the computer. I think best in that position, and it was a fitting one right now because correspondence with Admirer was looking more and more like a chess match. Every new move contained hidden traps and threats. Luckily, there was no clock forcing me to a quick reply. I did not start typing my response until I felt I had thoroughly considered all the implications of his email. The sound of two loud gongs barely disturbed my concentration.

Esteemed Admirer,

Would imitation truly be the first thing to cross people's minds about a novel that bears, as you say, my stamp in all respects except that it is signed by another name? Doesn't this contradict what you said in your last paragraph? If arrangements of this type are truly an open secret, then this explanation would come to mind too. It actually seems more probable.

But even if we stick to the sin of imitation which—we agree—has nothing to do with me, how do you intend to deal with the objections that will surely come your way? The certainty that your name will be sullied by accusations of imitation or even plagiarism cannot leave you unmoved.

(By the way, once the book comes out, your name will be a known quantity. So why do you hide it from me?)

Finally, at the risk of sounding even more naïve, I must ask how you discovered other examples of hiring a ghostwriter's services. How does one hear about them? Isn't it in the best interests of both parties to keep it all a secret? And wouldn't it be wiser to hide the unreliability of such arrangements from the person you are trying to get to consent to it?

Sincerely,
Writer

The first of the two new emails was from P-0 and the second was from Banana.

Dear Felix,—wrote P-0

Forgive me for not making myself clear. I completely understand how confusing my idea must have seemed, set out so succinctly. If it is any consolation, that's what I thought too when it first crossed my mind. But it is basically quite simple, although certainly unusual. It is based on reversing the natural order. Normally, the original work first appears and then the pastiche. But, I asked myself, does it necessarily have to be like that? Isn't it when literature leaves the well-trodden path that it advances? What stands in the way of the pastiche coming out first and then the original work on which it is based? Nothing, as far as I can see, except the two authors' readiness to take part in an unusual experiment. I am completely prepared for it and am confident that you too will see it as a challenge worthy of your reputation.

Sincerely yours,
P-0

Confused, I reread the message to make certain I had properly understood. I saved it mechanically, engrossed in formulating a response, and then started to write.

Dear P-0,

I'm afraid I still don't fully understand. You expect me to write an original based on the pastiche that you have previously written. But that cannot be. The order is essential. This would not be an original but actually a pastiche of a pastiche. And not a regular pastiche but one that is not modeled after any original.

In addition, there is the matter of the author's name. If you continue to sign with my name, even as a pseudonym, it would turn out that I myself was writing a pastiche of a pastiche of my own nonexistent work. I am not afraid of a challenge, of course, but isn't this too great an advancement for literature?

Sincerely yours,
Felix

How could he come up with something so complicated, I wondered as I sent the email. Really, a pastiche of a pastiche. But when I gave it more thought, why was I surprised? What he had done before was not so very different: signing a pastiche with the original author's name. What made me get involved in all of this? Now, of course, it was too late to wonder. Presumably my polite reply would let him know that I no longer wanted to be part of his machinations. If he continued to insist, I would have to take off the kid gloves and tell him point blank.

The same thing goes for Banana, I thought, opening her message. With her, however, there were not many items of clothing left to take off.

Dear Felix,

I have an idea why you are reluctant to help me. It's my fault for not mentioning it right away. I thought it was obvious. How could it be any other way? After you write the pivotal chapter, you will clearly have full rights to be the co-author of my literary debut. Denying you that right would be the same as my not acknowledging your undeniable paternity of my only child.

The comparison with paternity is more fitting than it might seem considering what happened after you stood up and turned towards me with nothing on your front. I stood up as well—how could I sit at a moment like that, even in my dream?—and suddenly realized that I was strangely dressed too. I had failed to notice it because I, unlike you, had clothes on my front. But not on my back. . . .

I was filled with unease, but not because of my bare backside, as one might think. I did not even try to hide it. On the contrary. As I turned my back and you came up to me, the only thing that discomforted me was the fact that I was not in the least embarrassed. I was still burning

with the ecstasy you brought me with your enchanting,
although one-fingered, playing at the keyboard . . .

Yours alone,
Banana

I drummed my fingers on the edge of the desk. That is what I do when something angers me. This was the last straw. What kid gloves? If this was what she wanted, we'd strip off everything. I had just clicked on the icon to reply to Banana's email, when a racket arose behind my back. If I had not known what was going on, I might have thought I was being robbed and burglars were tearing apart the living room and dining room.

That was indeed the first thing that crossed my mind soon after Felix moved into my life. On a similar morning, I had been sitting unsuspectingly at the computer just like this when a ruckus broke out in another area of the apartment. I rushed over, wondering how the burglars had managed to get in since the door was locked—and what a sight I beheld. The kitten was tearing around as though in a fit, climbing on the drapes, jumping on the table and the backs of the armchair and couch, dashing like crazy in all directions.

Had I brought a rabid animal into the house? I grabbed the wireless telephone, rushed into the bathroom and quite unnecessarily double-locked the door. I called the vet and asked for help in a terrified voice. Before he had heard me out, he started to laugh. I did not know whether I should join him, since everything was much less dangerous than it seemed, or be embarrassed for having made a fool of myself.

Like all happy-go-lucky cats, Felix lets off steam twice a day. After he has had his fill of sleeping and eating, he has to find a way to release the excess energy that has built up. I came out of the bathroom cautiously, just in case, even though his brief show was already over. A completely calm kitten was waiting for me in front of the door. He must have found it strange when I avoided petting him a little while longer, since I usually pet him whenever I can.

I soon got used to his boisterous behavior and even started taking part in it. Felix was happy to have company in his games. I would chase him, trying to catch him, which he found the greatest fun, but he was so fast that I looked like a clumsy clown. I realized that I would have to stop pursuing him not only because of the daily racket which, although of short duration, surely must bother the neighbors, but also because I almost hurt myself twice. First I fell on the armchair and turned it over and then I stumbled on the upturned corner of the rug and barely avoided hitting my head on the radiator.

Chance helped me tone down my participation in Felix's games. Each of the curtains on the windows in my study has three white plastic rods that keep it evenly stretched. I take them out of their long, thin pockets before I put the curtains in the washing machine. Once when I was taking out one of the rods, the tomcat was nearby. I waved the rod inadvertently in front of him and he was thrilled to death, clumsily trying to catch the white apparition oscillating before his eyes.

This was how one of the curtains came to lose its third rod after having been washed and Felix acquired the perfect toy. It was a relief for me too. I did not have to run after him anymore when he had an attack of excess energy. I would sit in the armchair and wiggle the rod on the carpet. This resulted in other benefits as well: less damage to the drapes and furniture in the living room from the cat's claws.

Felix's crazy fits started to last longer. He never grew weary of hunting the rod as long as I waved it in front of him. When I finally stopped, he would wrap himself around my legs, meow or even stand in front of my monitor to let me know he still felt like playing. I had no choice but to indulge him, even though after half an hour of waving I was quite bored.

Who knows how this clash between his perseverance and my boredom would have ended if chance had not intervened again. As I drew the rod in front of the tomcat, at one moment I accidently pushed it under the carpet. I was just about to take it out when I wondered what would happen if I left it hidden there.

What followed was an unexpected and favorable turn of events. Felix no longer needed me as a playmate. He was completely engrossed in trying to extricate the rod by himself. Even when it was clear that he would not succeed, he waited patiently by the edge of the rug for it to emerge.

I was grateful that Felix's hunting instinct had kicked in and spared me from wasting time, but I was also ill at ease. This did not really seem fair, like I had tricked him. In order to ease my conscience, I resisted the temptation to stick the rod under the carpet right away and still played with him for at least a quarter of an hour.

As I was playing with Felix now, circling the rod in front of the armchair, the gong sounded twice from my study. I did not stop playing, though. As always, the cat's persistence made me smile. He was able to chase the circling prey until his head spun. If I did not change the direction of the circle and briefly let him grab his prey, he would really be dizzy.

His delight now rubbed off on me and calmed my initial annoyance with Banana. Indeed, I was still determined not to let her ensnare me in her crafty plan, but the strong words I was intending to use were replaced by something milder.

When I estimated that Felix had released sufficient energy, I slid the rod deep under the carpet and headed back to my study. I flinched at the door when a new gong rang out. What a day, I thought once again, sitting at my desk, while lively scratching came from behind me.

Before I started to answer Banana, I glanced briefly at my virtual mailbox. The incoming emails were, in order, from Pandora, OpenSea and P-0.

Dear Banana,

I cannot be the co-author of a work that I did not help create. There is no paternity. Your fictional child has only a mother. You will have to bring it into the world by yourself. As I have already told you, even with the greatest willingness, I am unable to help you with it.

Sincerely,
Felix

As I saved and then sent the message, I thought that I might have been a bit hard on her. But no, it was better this way. If I kept the kid gloves on, the quibbling would draw out endlessly. Now she wouldn't insist any longer, I should think.

I opened Pandora's message.

Dear Mr. Felix,

How magnanimous of you! Only the greatest writer can be that!

Unfortunately, there is no hope for Albert. Even modern veterinary science is powerless before advanced old age. They might be able to prolong his life briefly, but at the price of considerable suffering. The poor thing has already suffered too much, however . . .

I will be eternally thankful for your offer of support and assistance in the difficult hours after Albert leaves us, but will certainly not abuse your wonderful kindness. I have already made all the necessary preparations. Perhaps, in my first days of solitude, I might write you more often. Please do not take this amiss. I have no one else to write to except you. There is no need to reply to each one of my emails. It will be enough to know that you have received it and read it . . .

Both Albert and I are indebted to you for your generous consent to write a novel about him. I haven't the least doubt that it will come from the depths of your heart. Just like all the rest of your beautiful books, of course. You might not believe me, but when I told Albert the good news, it had the effect of a miracle drug. I swear that he perked up, albeit briefly. If only I had ventured to ask you earlier: were it already written, your novel alone could prolong his life without suffering. Albert would not let himself die while I was reading it to him, and I would do it slowly, perhaps one paragraph a day . . .

I can barely wait for it to be finished. I will read it out loud, imagining that Albert is with me, listening. It will be as though he lived twice: in your wonderful novel and in reality.

Words fail me to express the enormous gratitude that Albert and I owe you.

With my deepest admiration,
Pandora

I'd have to take off the kid gloves here too. Well, maybe only halfway. Owing to Pandora's difficult situation, she simply might have overlooked the fact that I had agreed to write a story, not a novel. Even when people are overcome by lesser difficulties, they tend to see what suits them and not what really is. Indeed, I should have put greater emphasis on the fact that it was a story. That would have avoided any misunderstanding. I had better repair that oversight. Politely, of course, but in no uncertain terms.

Dear Mrs. Pandora,

You have conferred on me the highest compliment that a writer can receive. Indeed, what loftier expectation can there be of literature than to lessen the undue suffering in this world. If only you had informed me earlier that my story might bring Albert relief, I would have set to work without a moment's hesitation. Who knows, it might even turn into a novella. Unfortunately, despite the greatest willingness to help your dog in these difficult hours, I am hindered by my inadequate writing skills. I would give anything to be able to write quickly. Unfortunately, I am the type of writer who creates at a snail's pace. Several days would be necessary for a short story and a novella would stretch out for weeks if not months. All I can hope is that once the story is finished, it will bring a little consolation to you at least, if it is unable to help poor Albert . . .

With my deepest respects,
Felix

There, "story" was clearly written three times. All right, I did mention "novella" twice, but as a possibility, not a promise. In any case, regardless of the length of the story, I could always call it a novella. Furthermore, I did not tie myself to a short deadline, although I would try not to drag it out too long. Particularly if a flood of inspiration miraculously replaced the drought.

And now to see the circumstances in which Open-Sea would prefer a pseudonym to his beloved name. I saved Pandora's message and my reply and then opened his email.

If I wrote something that did not seem at all like mine. To have a bit of fun with the critics.

OpenSea's annoyance with the critics increased after every novel. There were considerably fewer reviews than he expected and the rare ones lacked not only enthusiasm but insight, to put it mildly. He read excerpts to me wrathfully, never ceasing to be amazed at the decline in literary criticism. The reviewers seemed to have lost their feel for great works. In the end, he concluded that the best thing would be to start reviewing his own books. This was not unseemly; he knew them better than anyone.

He was somewhat consoled by the long letters he received from three ladies after every book was published. They were delighted with his novels and showered them with praise. He tried to talk the editors of some small journals into publishing them, without success. In the end, he bought a large binder and turned it into an album. He got a hold of a photograph of each reader and pasted it next to their letters. The borders were decorated with colorful drawings of little flowers and butterflies.

What do you mean, did not seem like yours?—I asked him. *Like whose?*

Just as I opened P-0's email, I jumped at a new gong. I glanced at my virtual mailbox, saw that the message was from Admirer and then returned to the one that had arrived before it.

Dear Felix,

I agree completely. It would be unfitting for me to sign your name to pastiches of your as-yet-unwritten works. But since I am still hopeful that you will agree to write the originals after the fact, so they can be published together with my pastiches written before the fact, it would also be unfitting for me to sign the joint work with just my name. There are two possibilities: both of us sign as the au-

thors or we use a pseudonym. The first one has an obvious drawback. It would be quite understandable if you as a reputable author would rather not share authorship with a beginner, even though, of course, your name would be first on the cover and written in larger letters. As far as I can see, all that is left is a pseudonym.

Sincerely yours,
P-O

He did not seem to understand me either. Or did not want to understand me. The crucial issue here was not how we were going to sign this imbroglio with the pastiches. The point was that I did not want to have anything to do with it, even under a pseudonym. It seemed like the gloves would have to come off again. All right, maybe not all the way. Three-quarters might be enough.

Dear P-O,

If you are going to sign what is actually an original work with a pseudonym, then there is actually no need for me to write the original after the fact. It seems much more fitting for you to do it yourself. You are so skilled at writing pastiches of my stories that no one will suspect that my so-called original was not written by me. As far as I am concerned, I will neither confirm nor deny their authenticity. Even though your name will not be on the cover, that fact will certainly not decrease your pleasure in knowing that you are the sole author of the book.

Sincerely yours,
Felix

I reread the email before I saved it. I always do that. Often there is something to correct or touch up. This time it seemed that I had gotten it all right. Even so, as I sent it I was haunted by the feeling that things were not headed in the right direction. Instead of getting disentangled, they were becoming even more convoluted. Not only with P-0 but with the others as well. Who could tell what awaited me in Admirer's new message. As I opened it, the gong forced me to flinch once more. I glanced at my virtual mailbox, saw that it was Banana again, sighed and then went back to Admirer.

Highly Esteemed Writer,

Naturally it is in the interests of both parties for the arrangement to remain secret. It is actually more in the interests of the writer. Only his name can be sullied. The other party is not a known writer so his literary reputation is not in danger. His moral reputation might be, but if he had any scruples, he would probably not get involved in such a business.

In spite of these circumstances, many such cases become public knowledge because the writers leak the news, believe it or not. Surely you wonder what makes them denounce themselves. If you give it some thought, the answer is quite predictable: vanity. They cannot bear to see their work come out under someone else's name. They prefer dishonor to letting someone steal their thunder.

Such twists, which do damage to everyone, are possible because of flaws in the contracts. In the meantime, these have improved in one essential respect. The work does not come out under the name of the one placing the order but under a pseudonym. An elegant solution that removes all the drawbacks!

In particular, the matter of imitation or plagiarism is no longer an issue. Now there is a much simpler explanation for the same writing style. The author himself is hiding behind the pseudonym. And how could he imitate or even worse, plagiarize himself?

The writer, of course, must not admit publicly that he has signed with a pseudonym, but he does not have to deny it either. He will diplomatically refrain from commenting, just as he would not comment if no arrangement existed and he had just decided to use a pseudonym. Why would he do that unless there was some reason to hide his real name?

This also removes the problem of vanity. The book does not come out under the name of a real person so there is no reason for the writer to be hurt and do a disservice to himself and his business partner by exposing the arrangement. He is also forced to be discreet by a new clause in the contract providing high damages to the other party should he do it nonetheless.

Finally, this also protects the identity of the partner. Since his name will not appear on the cover, he can remain anonymous.

Sincerely,
Admirer

I took up my chess-playing position once again and spent several minutes like that, staring at the white screen waiting to be filled with my reply. Felix interrupted my concentration briefly. He had given up lying in wait for the rod and silently returned to the study. He hung about my feet a bit and then headed off somewhere, letting me think once again. I finally started to type.

Esteemed Admirer,

Although it seems like a handy solution, a pseudonym still does not remove all the dilemmas. Let's say that the writer, who has decided to take part in something dishonorable, has the least reason to be dissatisfied. At least he can tacitly pretend that the work is his. (Just as it is, strictly speaking). But what about the other party? What does he get with a pseudonym? If he does not have a chance to sign his own name, what connects him to the book? Indeed, he might claim that he is hiding behind the pseudonym, but who would have reason to believe him? And if he cannot convince anyone that he is the author, why would he pay for the authorship?

Since we are on the subject of authorship, a more important question arises. Why would the author sell it?

Sincerely,
Writer

Just as I saved the email, Felix suddenly materialized on my desk again. This time there was nothing he could spill, but the jump did not turn out to be totally harmless. The edge of the keyboard stopped his slide, but he lost his balance and stretched out full length across the keys. The open email window instantly disappeared from the screen and two others appeared. As I lifted Felix off the keys, the speakers let out a stream of sharp screeching.

Luckily, this time everything was saved, but on another similar occasion I had lost a full two and a half pages of text. At first I had been extremely angry with Felix and even scolded him harshly, but soon regretted it, realizing that I was in fact to blame. Nothing would have been lost if I had saved the text more often instead of putting it off just because I wanted to outsmart the computer. And I deserved to pay the price for my irrational behavior.

Chaos instantaneously ensued, but still I had to laugh at the horrified tomcat's failure to understand what had befallen him, even though this occurred almost daily. As I put the screen in order and tried to stop the screeching, Felix jumped onto the printer and then onto the varnished shelf with the speakers and the brass flowerpot.

I knew what would come next. He raised his head towards the long, bent leaves of the yucca, sniffed them briefly and then started to chew the already tattered edges of the lowest one. For a while I had tried to break him of the habit, but he was persistent and I could not move the plant to another place because it got the most sunlight there.

The vet explained to me that cats periodically eat plants to help their digestion. Indeed, he had yet to hear that they liked yucca. But, then, why wouldn't they, he wondered. Truly, what could be better for a healthy life than a yucca, the tree of life, he added, smiling at his witticism. He suggested that if I wanted to save the plant, I should put grains of wheat in a dish with water and let them sprout. Felix would probably like that better.

But he had only sniffed inquisitively here and there at the wheat grass without even taking a nibble and continued to chew on the yucca. I was already resigned to the fact that Felix would ruin it, when some sort of truce was reached. The yucca sacrificed one leaf to the cat and in return he spared the others. He only nibbled on the one that was easiest to reach. The leaf had turned a bit yellow and wilted, but was still holding its own. The others seemed to turn a more vibrant green.

I watched Felix for a moment as he enjoyed the yucca, then sent the email to Admirer and opened Banana's, sensing more trouble.

Dear Felix,

Have I misjudged you? I must believe that I haven't. Would a writer such as you act like a heartless seducer from a cheap romance novel? No, that does not seem at all possible. The noble and sensitive man that I still think you to be would never turn his back on a lady after she had turned her bare back to him. Even if only in a dream, but does this make it any less real? Of all people, a master of fiction should be the last one to challenge the reality of what we write or dream.

Particularly when it is as fervent as our coupling. Its memory causes greater trembling than the reminiscence of real events and I can still see your flushed face when it was all over and the missing parts of our clothing appeared on us.

(As though this was not tense enough, a new gong heightened the excitement of the moment.)

That is the face that mightily disavows the words with which you now renounce your paternity. Why did you write them when we both know they are not true? You are certainly capable of making an invaluable contribution to our common offspring. You have already shown me with great conviction. The fruit of our rapture is already in my womb and is only waiting to be born. Why would you want it to stay unborn?

I have thought this over and only one explanation comes to mind. I offered you the co-authorship of our child. For it to carry both your name and mine. That seemed the fairest to me. Is that what bothers you? Do you want it to carry only its father's name? I readily agree, even though I imagined you as someone without patriarchal preconceptions.

Or is it the other way around? Perhaps our son—don't ask me how I know it is a boy; a mother knows even without ultrasound—does not seem worthy of your name that you save for only legitimate children, your own books? If this is the case, I will understand as well, albeit with a heavy heart. What counts most is that our son comes into the world. I put that before everything, even pride. You do not have to acknowledge him as your progeny. Let him be a bastard. He will not receive my name either. Just so you don't think I am vain and vindictive. We will choose a pseudonym for him. A pretty one. Do you have any suggestions?

Still steadfastly yours,
Banana

I spent some time trying to figure out what—and how—I should reply to this, then concluded that the wisest thing would be no reply. What could I say, anyway? There clearly was no point in repeating that I was unable and did not want to do what she expected of me. However resolute my stand, for her it would be just a continuation of this nonsense about paternity, names and the bastard. She would probably interpret my silence in the same spirit, but at least I would be spared from needlessly writing.

I saved her email and then looked at my virtual mailbox.

Dear Mr. Felix,—wrote Pandora

You are humility itself! Only a writer truly crowned by this virtue would say of himself that he writes slowly, while he has written so many works and is still relatively young!

Please do not think that these words are meant to hurry you. Let your novel about Albert take the necessary time to be written. I will do my very best to be patient. Should it happen nonetheless that during the coming weeks I succumb to temptation and discreetly enquire how the novel is coming, please do not take me wrongly. There are days when it seems that my end has drawn nigh, that I will not live to see anything nice again. Pay no attention to my unbecoming curiosity. Write the novel at the pace your muse commands. I will certainly not allow the end to come too soon.

And now I owe you a great apology. I was so terribly thrilled when you agreed to grant my request that I overlooked the fact that it must have put you in an awkward situation. I thus hasten to remedy this unintentional embarrassment.

It is quite possible that you see this "commissioned" novel about Albert in a different light. While I have absolutely no doubt that it will be wonderfully written, there is a chance that it might not fit into your opus. I will completely understand if you want to set it apart in some way. Perhaps the most suitable way would be to write it under a pseudonym. Please do not hesitate in this regard. This will not bother me in the least. Does it matter whose name is on the cover of the novel if I know from whose heart it originates?

With my deepest admiration,
Pandora

I started counting. She had written "novel" five times. This was no misunderstanding. She could not have failed to note that I constantly mentioned story and only allowed a novella as a remote possibility. This was cunning. More subtle than Banana's to be sure, but still an attempt to get more than she could politely ask for. I would have preferred not to send a reply here either, but Pandora was something else. I would pretend not to notice her persistence, while persistently stressing it was a story.

Dear Mrs. Pandora,

The story about Albert will fit perfectly into my opus. For some time now I have been thinking of writing a story about a pet. Indeed, I have more experience with cats than dogs, but I would say that I have become thoroughly acquainted with dogs through your sketches about Albert and my humble self, so I do not foresee any difficulties. My sole regret is that the story will have been prompted by a sad occasion. In any case, I will be pleased to sign the story with my name. There is no reason to hide behind a pseudonym just for this story.

With my deepest respects,
Felix

There. Now we were tied. Any other time I would be horrified at repeating the same word five times in a short paragraph, but this was justified.

After I had saved and sent the email, I was struck by a coincidence. Although conspicuous, it had slipped by me because of my total absorption in the cunning web being spun around me. Almost simultaneously, all five people I had been corresponding with this morning had come up with the idea of a pseudonym. They all seemed to be in collusion, which was impossible of course. Not one of them knew about the others. Even though I could not be sure about Admirer, there was no cause for paranoid second thoughts.

Felix finished chewing on the yucca and jumped via the printer to the free area on my desk next to the keyboard. He stayed there, contemplating his next move. Often, like now, he does not know what to do with himself. Since nothing comes to mind most of the time, he simply sits there for a while staring blankly until his eyes start to close and then lies down wherever he happens to be. It might be much more comfortable a little farther away, but he clearly does not feel like moving.

My conscience always bothers me at such times. I feel it is my duty to entertain him and not let him be a lazybones. Once the tomcat stretches out, only the white rod can snap him out of his drowsiness. But if I got him going with it, I would lose at least half an hour and then I would feel guilty for wasting my own time.

Felix's unexpected decision not to stay on the desk spared my conscience on this occasion. As though suddenly remembering something important he had to do, he headed for the edge. He did not jump right away, though. He had to make preparations: first he took a good look at where he would jump, then he leaned forward a bit, tightened the muscles in his hind legs and started slowly rocking back and forth. The gong that rang out at that very moment was like the shot of a starting gun. I bounced on my chair and the tomcat jumped at least half a meter farther than he intended and collided with the—fortunately soft—footstool.

I grabbed the mouse angrily. My irritation only grew when I saw that the short email was from OpenSea. And my fury went up another notch when I read it.

Like yours. But a little out of whack. You are certainly aware that what you write simply begs to be parodied.

If I had not seen red, Felix would have had an easier time. As it was, I practically screamed at him when he started digging his claws into the footstool. I would have raised my voice under other circumstances too, but not this much. He received a scolding almost on a daily basis for such bad habits. Many parts of my furniture were ruined, the poor footstool in particular. It was tattered on two sides.

I had followed the vet's advice and brought him various objects that could replace the furniture. All he did was sniff inquisitively at the log, the doormat and the plush monkey, without a clue as to how he could use them. It did not even help when I used my own nails to show what was expected of him. He kept on scratching at his habitual places.

My shouting now sent him skulking behind the two-seater. Just as I was feeling sorry for venting my fury at OpenSea on poor Felix, sounds came from behind the couch that told me he had not taken my verbal assault to heart. He was not cringing back there, frightened and depressed, but had once again started sharpening his claws as though in defiance. All I could do was shrug my shoulders. I was consoled by the fact that the back of the two-seater was out of sight.

I had just saved OpenSea's email when a new gong rang out. This seemed to signal Felix finally to stop. I did not look at my virtual mailbox right away because anger still had the upper hand.

I suppose—I said in reply to OpenSea—*that I should be delighted that a literary giant has decided to suspend briefly the creation of his major works in order to parody the pitiful writing of my humble self.*

A new message from P-0 was waiting in my mailbox.

Dear Felix,

I am truly honored by the trust you have in my ability to write both the pastiches and their subsequent originals. I am also grateful at your readiness not to deny that they did not come from your pen. But even if I were to write them, it would not be the same as if you had. Your authentic presence in the book is more than essential. So, please don't hold it against me for not giving up on the idea of somehow getting you to take part in it. I am ready to make all kinds of concessions to ensure this. I would be willing to pay whatever price it takes ...

If, as I hope, you finally agree, I would venture to propose the pseudonym we could use to sign our joint work. I did not have to think twice. What could be more appropriate than your virtual nickname: Felix?

Sincerely yours,
P-0

This guy wouldn't give up. Well, fine. I would take advantage of a favorable circumstance to extricate myself from the whole predicament without further ado.

Dear P-0,

Please stop insisting (Gong!) *that I take part in writing your book. If it weren't for the fact that we have been on friendly terms for so long, I would be insulted by your mentioning "pay" and "price".*

It will be best (Gong!) *for both of us if you write your first book by yourself, and since that's the way it is, wouldn't it be more appropriate for you to sign it with your own pseudonym? It seems to me that P-0 is much more fitting for a pastiche of a pastiche than Felix.*

Sincerely yours,
Felix

The first email was from OpenSea and the second was from Banana. OpenSea would not normally be awake at this time of day. He went to bed very late and did not get up until after the stroke of noon. Sometimes he would give me a buzz on the phone after midnight to tell me that he had just sent an email. He never asked whether I had already gone to bed. It was understood that his message had priority over such trivialities.

For a long time I got up obligingly and turned on the computer, until he finally went too far. After he woke me up at twenty-five to four, I started unplugging the telephone before I went to bed. He held it against me, of course. I reminded him that he did the same thing at daybreak just before he went to bed, but he replied with a sniff that it was not, of course, the same thing.

For some reason OpenSea had, evidently, fallen asleep much earlier than usual last night. I wondered for a minute whether this had anything to do with the contents of his emails today, but I could not detect any link.

Actually—began his new message—*when I give it some thought, maybe the best thing would be if you were to write a parody of your own work. Then you would re-deem yourself a little and I wouldn't have to waste my time with it. You would sign it, of course, with a pseud-onym—even you can see that it would be foolish to parody yourself under your own name—but one that still points to you. The one you use here would work. That's the same name you gave your horrid animal, isn't it?*

My cheeks flushed with anger. I wasn't so hurt by his twisted suggestion that I parody myself or the barb that I should do it for the sake of redemption. The slur regarding Felix hit me the hardest. Only someone like OpenSea could call that sweet creature a "horrid ani-mal". Too bad the dog hadn't bitten him even harder.

I turned towards the two-seater and spotted Felix peeping out from behind it. He looked at me question-ingly to check whether I was still mad about his sharp-ening his claws. I got up quickly, went over to him, picked him up, held him in my arms and kissed him two or three times between the ears as I stroked his back. Soon he started purring softly. By his confused expression I would say he was wondering what he had done to deserve this sudden outpouring of affection.

Our cuddling would have lasted even longer if it hadn't been for another gong that interrupted us. I put Felix on the floor and went back to the computer. Be-fore I started to write a reply to OpenSea, I checked my virtual mailbox and saw Pandora's new message.

I don't see—I wrote to OpenSea—*what could get me to agree to something as idiotic as parodying myself. And even less to abusing my dear cat's name on such hogwash.*

I was still boiling with anger when I opened Banana's email. Unless she gives up on that nonsense, she'll get the same thing as OpenSea. I am a decent man, but everything has its limit.

Dear Felix,

My, what a reckless chatterbox I am! Forgive me, forgive me, forgive me. I completely understand why you didn't reply to my last message. Please believe that I had no intention of hurting you with that stupid question at the end. In my excitement it simply slipped out. Of course our son will be given the most beautiful of names! What could be more beautiful than his father's wonderful nickname—Felix?

Yours forever,
Banana

In spite of my anguish, a sudden thought made me laugh out loud. Felix glanced at me dubiously and then continued licking himself on the floor. If she had gotten it into her head that she would have a daughter, the baby would have to get Mama's wonderful nickname. And then my face darkened again.

This was completely out of control. She was becoming too familiar. Of course. She didn't want to be formal towards the father of her child. This was not mere cunning calculated to shift the burden of finishing a book that could not be finished. It seemed she believed what she imagined was true.

I spent a minute and a half holding my right forefinger above the keyboard, but nothing suitable came to mind. I could try to bring her to reason, but the chances seemed quite slim. On the other hand, I could not be rough with her anymore. One must show understanding towards someone who was clearly disturbed. But how could I pull it off? I could not agree with her. That way both of us would end up deranged.

I finally concluded that the best thing was to do what I had done last time. There would be no reply. I saved Banana's email and then opened Pandora's.

Dear Mr. Felix,

There is something I must ask you and my heart is sinking. You have already shown me such rare kindness by agreeing to write a novel about Albert. Only exceptional people are characterized by such generosity. The greatest writers. Then how ungrateful you must find my audacity in asking for something else on top of this immeasurable gift. My sole exoneration might be the truly difficult circumstances that compel me to do it.

I will be eternally in your debt if you would agree to sign the novel with a pseudonym. And a special one at that—the one with which you appear with Albert in my little stories.

Felix.

I beg you not to think that I ask this because I find your name unpleasant. Oh, quite the contrary. You have such a wonderful name. The problem, however, is that Albert does not know you (Gong!) by that name. Whenever I speak to him about you, every time I read him the stories where both of you appear, you are always Felix. And names are like smells with dogs: once they remember your smell, there can be no other. You will always be Felix for poor Albert. That is your singular smell.

Perhaps you might wonder whether it makes any difference what you smell like, since Albert will soon no longer be with us. Of course it does. Albert might be dead for others, but he will continue to live for me. I know that he will be overjoyed when he listens to me read Felix's wonderful novel about him. Please do not hold it against him, but the joy would be missing if the writer of the novel were someone quite unknown to him, even someone with a beautiful smell.

My humble request on Albert's behalf should by no

means put you in an awkward position. If for any reason it does not suit you to have one of your novels published under the pseudonym Felix, that must be duly respected. As far as I am concerned, the novel about Albert does not even have to be published. It will be more than enough if I receive it in manuscript form. This would make Albert and me feel even more pleased and honored. And even more grateful to our benefactor.

With my deepest respects,
Pandora

I felt another strong reaction coming on, but this time not a laugh. I held back lest I disturb Felix's innocent washing. This lady was not merely cunning. If that were all she was, she would have gone no further than the already brazen attempt to get me to write a novel. But expecting me to write a novel that would not be published and would merely serve to maintain a state of derangement, regardless of the sad occasion that caused it—that would only cross the mind of someone who had lost their mind.

It was high time to pull out of this predicament. Luckily, Pandora had provided an opening. She might not acknowledge any other pretext, but this one she would because it held to the logic of her derangement.

Dear Mrs. Pandora,

I am inconsolable!
If Felix is the only smell by which Albert recognizes me, then we are in serious trouble. Of all the pseudonyms in the world, that is the only one I cannot use. I gave Felix my solemn promise. He would never forgive me if I betrayed him. Worse than that. Who knows what he might do to take his revenge. You do not know him. He might even raise a paw against himself.

Shame prevented me from admitting it to you earlier, but unlike Albert, Felix is no fan of fiction, least of all mine. In fact, he finds it extremely offensive. Disgusting, actually. Don't ask me why. As we know, there's no accounting for taste.

I did everything I could to bring him round, but all in vain. I even proposed that I write a novel about him and was prepared to sign it with his name. He shuddered at the former and was totally horrified at the latter. He stopped eating until I solemnly promised that his name would never appear in one of my books, either on the cover or inside.

So what's to be done? You be the judge. If my losing Felix will bring Albert back to you, I will make that sacrifice.

With my deepest respects,
Felix

I sent the message and headed for my virtual mailbox, but the cursor didn't make it. Halfway there I suddenly noted another coincidence and stopped. It was a continuation of the previous one. Not only had they all agreed to putting a pseudonym into play, but they had chosen the same one: Felix. One coincidence might be accidental but two were too much.

Before my paranoia had a chance to mushroom, it dawned on me that the choice was actually not strange. What could be more natural than to propose my pseudonym in the virtual world? It simply sprang to mind. OpenSea had an additional reason. He wanted it to be easy to conclude who was parodying himself—among those who did not know me as Felix, word would quickly spread as to who was hiding behind the pseudonym—plus he had also had a chance to say something mean about my tomcat. He knew that would really smart.

Even if my pseudonym were not the obvious choice, the possibility that some sort of conspiracy was behind everything seemed too far-fetched. I would finally have to reject the idea simply because there was no way it could be explained. Indeed, it was completely unfathomable that five such different people would join forces just to have a bit of fun with me. Actually, there were only four, not five. Admirer had not mentioned Felix. How could he since he knew nothing about my pseudonym or my cat?

I shrugged my shoulders and then finished the move. It was his email waiting for me in the mailbox.

Highly Esteemed Writer,

I'm afraid that I cannot tell you why I want to buy the authorship of your book. There are reasons that must (Gong!) *remain secret, as must my name.*

Rest assured, however, that my motives are honorable, regardless of how dishonorable this might seem to you. You haven't (Gong!) *the slightest reason to worry. Your interests will be fully protected by the contract. I would also add—and by my honor, although I am aware that this guarantee is insufficient under the given circumstances.*

Furthermore, in order to remove any fears about tarnishing your reputation, I pledge not to make a single change to the manuscript. I will follow it to the last punctuation mark, even though as a rule the customer has a free hand with such arrangements. In addition, I am more than ready to let you (Gong!) *choose the pseudonym. I suppose that Felix might suit you, but should you wish something else, it will be followed to the letter.*

Finally, there is the matter of your motives. You have told me several times already that you would never agree to something (Gong!) *you deemed improper regardless of the price. I completely understand your repugnance. If I were in your shoes, I too would consider such a proposal insulting. Nevertheless, do not be too hasty in making the final decision. Offers exist for everything, this included, that cannot be refused . . .*

   Sincerely,
   Admirer

I don't know which upset me the most—recoiling from the speakers' rapid-fire explosions or what I read. Why not turn down the sound at least when I was in the study? What difference would it make if I forgot to turn it up when I went elsewhere in the apartment? Would the earth stop spinning if I didn't find out the instant a message arrived? Of course it wouldn't, but just try convincing an addict of that. I was ashamed of myself.

Admirer's words only increased my shame. Did he think I was a prostitute? Well, not exactly a streetwalker, but was that any consolation? Actually, this was worse than prostitution, a profession that entails loaning your body, not selling it. Temporarily, for an hour or a night. Then it's yours again. This was permanently divesting oneself of a literary work, something dearer to a writer than his own body. A book stays young and beautiful forever and a body ages and weakens.

And then that cynical conclusion that everything has its price. I felt like terminating my correspondence with him at once by snapping that he was greatly mistaken. He could not buy me at any price. I was not for sale. Or maybe it would be best not to reply at all. Such cheapening deserved nothing but the deepest scorn. But I had to postpone this severance. Something in his letter required an explanation.

The fifth mention of Felix.

Esteemed Admirer,
(I hesitated briefly whether to leave out the intro-

ductory address or put something unfriendly instead of "esteemed", but that would only indicate how much he had hurt me.)

What makes you think that the pseudonym Felix would be most suitable? Do we know each other?

Sincerely,
Writer

I sent the email, but before I had time to open my virtual mailbox, Felix appeared on my desk again. This time he landed with surprising skill and stopped before he ran into anything. Even he was amazed at this feat and stayed for a few moments at the spot where his sliding ended. Then, tail raised proudly, he headed towards the space between the keyboard and monitor.

This is where I keep my cell phone, a small calculator and the remote control for the air conditioning. Felix is no longer light, but he cannot do too much damage as he walks gingerly over the three devices.

Once he stepped on the phone's recall button. I would not have noticed if the owner of the number hadn't called me on my fixed phone to ask why I had been as silent as the grave on my cell for the past eleven minutes. He did not tell me why he had waited so long to find out. In any case, since then I keep it turned off.

Felix's paws made wondrous calculations on the calculator. After one such pass, the little display magically showed a figure whose first four digits matched the number pi. The calculator was otherwise a relic from my pre-computer days. I still preferred to use it instead of the virtual calculator on the screen.

The remote control was also a problem. After I got home one sizzling hot day last summer, I almost fainted. It was hotter inside than outside, even though I had left the air conditioning on. Felix had managed to change the setting and turned the cooling to heating. I put an end to that by removing the batteries.

Now the tomcat stopped in front of the monitor, blocking it almost completely. This was what I was afraid of. If he decided to sit there, it would not be brief. Once I had to wait a full thirty-five minutes for him to move so I could continue writing. I breathed a sigh of relief when he moved on some fifteen seconds later.

He reached the end of the monitor and stopped again, pondering what to do next. If he decided to go back, I had another problem in store. He never went the same way. For some strange reason, he preferred to go along the very narrow strip between the keyboard and the edge of the desk. It was wide enough for other cats, but not for clumsy Felix. He lost his balance almost without fail and fell in my lap or on the keyboard.

The latter possibility was dangerous. Panic filled me at the thought of the four new messages in my mailbox that had not been saved. The chances were nil of them being spoiled by the accidental fall of any other cat or even a larger animal, but experience had taught me that Felix did not go by the laws of probability but by Murphy's law.

I sighed once again when he headed for the laptop. He sniffed it a bit and then sat on the black surface, staring out at the blue sky through the yucca leaves. There was no time to hesitate. He might change his mind. I quickly took the mouse to the virtual mailbox. The emails had arrived in this order: OpenSea, Banana, P-0 and Pandora. I sighed with relief once I had saved them, even though Felix no longer presented any danger. In the meantime he had stretched out and his eyes were already half-closed.

It's better for you to parody yourself than for me to do it—wrote OpenSea. *You will certainly be kinder to yourself. Go ahead and include the cat, since you care so much*

*about it. A parody is where it belongs, not in an apartment.
If you're stubborn, though, there's a cure for that too.*

I let out a growl, causing Felix to start and look at me
wide-eyed. His eyelids only started closing again when
I stroked him several times. The feel of his thick, soft
fur had a calming effect on me, easing my first impulse
to give OpenSea what he deserved. A four-letter word.

Then I thought of threatening to erase our entire
correspondence if he didn't let up. He would probably
call my bluff. He knew that my email collecting mania
would never let me erase a single one. He certainly had
made fun of me on that account. Why do you keep all
that garbage? Not all of it was garbage, though. His
messages were the exception, of course.

I finally decided not to reply. In any case, what could
I say to the vague threat at the end of his email? I was
completely uninterested in the cure he had in mind.
If he felt like parodying my humble self, let him. He
certainly could not talk me into doing it.

I moved to the next message.

Felix,—began Banana coldly

*So, that's it. No reply. As though you have nothing to
do with this. The guy did what he felt like and now he's
washed his hands. Let the poor young woman rack her
brains about what to do next. Who's to blame for her
naïveté? And I was naïve when I let the cheap song of a
one-fingered pianist drive me wild.*

*But you are terribly mistaken if you think my naïveté
is endless. Even though I was besotted, I had enough presence of mind to provide for myself should you leave me in
the lurch. You'll soon see how. You will acknowledge your
paternity whether you like it or not.*

Banana

What paternity, I wanted to shout, but held back so as not to upset Felix, who was now napping. Everything was mixed up in Banana's head. Fascinated by the cliché of a pregnant young woman abandoned by her lover, she had lost sight of the fact that no one was pregnant here. It was not that I refused to acknowledge any paternity but that I did not want to take part in any paternity.

Let her find someone else to be her son's father. Or better yet, let her be both papa and mama, if she could not do without a papa. That's the most natural thing in literature. I toyed briefly with the idea of trying to bring her to her senses, but it would not be worth it. This had already gone too far. I would remain silent. Why should I try if, as she said, she'd already provided for herself? Let's just see what she's concocted, I thought.

I opened P-0's email.

Dear Felix,

I apologize for the misunderstanding. I did not literally mean "pay" and "price" of course. I realize that this is no way to get the collaboration of a great writer. But there might be another way. I will spare you from further insistence that we write a book together, but I will not give up hope. Miracles do happen. Indeed, not always by themselves. Sometimes they need a little assistance . . .

Please do not hold it against me, but I think I will sign as Felix nonetheless. I would prefer to do so with your blessing, but if you refuse, you leave me no choice. P-0 seems quite unliterary, like some ordinary code compared to the dignified Felix, and it does not indicate my indebtedness to you. And I repay my debts . . .

Sincerely yours,
P-0

I had no reason to reply here either. Even though P-0's twisted fabrication did not fall short of Banana's, at least I did not have to bring him to his senses. It was important for him to realize that he could not get me involved in all that. He could hope and believe in miracles all he wanted. Spontaneous or assisted.

Plus, he could keep the pseudonym Felix. It was much more charming than P-0. In any case, how could I prevent him? I did not have a copyright to the name. Besides, what did it matter if people thought I was the author? I could always deny it if it raised any dust. Or wisely refrain from commenting, if the book was well-received.

Only Pandora was left.

Dear Mr. Felix,

This is terrible. You have completely devastated me with what you said about Felix. Is it possible that he feels that way about your wonderful writing? He alone, of all the animals in the world, who enjoys the privilege of living with you? Is there any greater betrayal than having your nearest and dearest turn their back on you?

You are too indulgent towards him when you say there is no accounting for taste. He has no taste at all. If he does not like what you write, I can just imagine what kind of literature attracts him.

But why am I surprised? I know what cats are like. Why do you think I took a dog after Leopold? Because Leopold was no different than Felix. Cats do not have the slightest an appreciation of art. I did everything I could to engender a love of literature in him, since he had no feeling for music and painting. I read and read to him, but nothing got through. We should not speak ill of the dead, but even so I will tell you his shame. Cartoons were all that interested him and the silliest ones at that. Just imagine.

Even though I am aware that your tomcat does not deserve you in the least, I would never think of accepting the sacrifice that you gallantly offered. I cannot let you break the promise you made to Felix and end up without him. Cats are terribly stubborn. He would certainly make good on his threat to kill himself.

What else can I do? I thought about suggesting that you hide the fact from Felix that you will sign the novel about Albert with his name. Since there will be only one copy of the book and I will have it, he would never find out. But it was a foolish thought. You are not only a great writer but also, of course, an honest man whose conscience would never let him get involved in such duplicity.

Is there any other solution? Perhaps one, but it is not honorable either. If only despair weren't compelling me to take that route. Please forgive me . . .

With my deepest respects,
Pandora

I did not understand why I was supposed to forgive her. I could have asked what other dishonorable solution she had in mind, but since it clearly did not include me, it was none of my concern. This was the chance I was waiting for: to extricate myself from the whole thing without further ado. She had not asked any questions so I did not have to reply.

I erased the four messages from my virtual mailbox. It was strange to see it empty. I could not remember so many exchanges in one morning. Well, now it would probably stop. I had reached an end of sorts with all of them. It was about time, anyway. I could always exchange emails later, but I only write at this time of day, and not much of it was left.

I closed the email program and opened the word processor. But I did not look at a single file. There was nothing in the folder I had entitled "Ongoing". It has been empty for quite some time. Drought is not just OpenSea's trouble.

I set my elbows by the keyboard, placed one hand over the other and rested my nose on my fingers, staring hazily at the virginal whiteness of the monitor. I could stay in that position for a long time. Even long after it was certain that no inspiration would be forthcoming to defile that whiteness.

When this certainty becomes apparent, the soul quickly drops in price. But what's the good when there are no buyers even at a pittance? Silence is the Devil's ultimate ridicule. While his humiliating silence echoes all around, crazy ideas go through a writer's mind: coaxing someone into parodying himself, laying one's hands on the gist of a story through an erotic nightmare, tangling an inextricable knot of pastiches of pastiches, finagling a novel with only one copy.

Assuming the role of the Devil.

But this time I did not go over the brink. Not because I had a brainwave. I didn't. I was saved by a pigeon.

It landed on the satellite antenna on the other side of the window and started to coo. Felix jerked out of his sound sleep at the very same moment. His inactive hunting instincts came powerfully alive. He slid off the laptop and sneaked up silently to the printer, which served as cover. He peered out briefly to spot his prey. When he caught sight of it, he started to emit noises.

I'd been alarmed when I'd heard them for the first time, not long after I brought Felix home. I had no idea that they were coming from him. Then, as now, what I heard behind my back when a bird suddenly stopped at the window resembled the low growl of a dog. I turned around to see Felix in an unusual position. He was lying on the floor, front paws extended, head lowered and haunches slightly raised, as though getting ready to run.

When this happened the bird's instincts would also kick in and it usually flew off before he got moving, but once he was too fast. Not fast enough to catch his prey, but fast enough not to stop in time.

I jumped to the window in a panic and looked down the three-floor abyss. There was Felix, lying motionless in a hedge. As I ran down the stairs, too impatient to wait for the elevator, I was certain that there was no way he could have survived the fall. Other cats might have nine lives, but Felix had barely been given one.

I found him standing by the hedge, perplexed. He clearly had no idea what had happened. And how lucky he was. He acted as though he had walked there at his leisure and not fallen. As I carried him back to the apartment, feeling him all over to check whether anything was broken, I sweet-talked and scolded him in the same breath.

For a long time after that I kept the window closed, even though I did not like it. I had kept it ajar even in the coldest weather, and with the slightest fair weather it would be wide open. Finally, I could not stand it anymore. I had to find another solution.

It was simple but heavy-handed and could perhaps have been avoided since Felix had most likely learned his lesson. Would he let himself get into the same scrape twice? Who could say for sure? He might have become more cautious, but not more agile. While he was getting ready, as now, to tear after a bird near the window, I would clap my hands together. The bird would fly off and he would end up the loser, but at least I did not have to check how many lives he had left.

This is what I did now. The pigeon took wing and Felix jumped onto the printer as though wanting to fly off after it. But he didn't. He just watched in frustration, still growling, as it flew away. When it disappeared from view, he turned towards me and gave me a deeply reproving glance. I bore up stoically under it, as usual. Let him be angry with me. It was more important for his head to remain on his shoulders.

He did not go back to the laptop but jumped off the desk instead, not wanting to have anything more to do with me. I took it calmly and went back to the monitor. I stared briefly at the hopeless whiteness, then reconciled myself to the inevitable and turned off the word processor. Another unproductive day.

I soon heard Felix scratching on the rug. My placidity obviously irritated him even more. He expected me to apologize and sweet-talk him. He knew that I always scolded him for ruining the rug like that. He had badly damaged it in one place. Now he was simply being defiant. But he would not provoke me even if he dug a hole. I kept my back resolutely turned on him.

It took the sound of the gong to get him to stop. I turned around and watched him leave the study. His waving tail indicated that he was still ruffled. But he wouldn't be for long. He would soon forget the bird and what I had done. Felix did not hold a grudge.

As I opened the email program, I wondered which of my four correspondents had decided to add a postscript. But it wasn't any of them. I had a fifth correspondent today, one who had briefly slipped my mind. The conversation with him was not yet over.

Highly Esteemed Writer,

I do not have a good answer to the question of whether we know each other. If I were to confirm that, I might jeopardize my identity, which I told you must remain a secret. If I were to deny it, you probably would not believe me. You would certainly be gnawed by a worm of doubt. So it's best not to give any answer.

Let's just say instead that—whether or not I know you personally—I have done my homework. Can you hold that against me? This is a serious business that one does not engage in unprepared. As far as Felix is concerned, I know that there are two Felixes in your life. One is your virtual pseudonym that you use in more personal correspondence. And one is also the name of your cat.

And now let's get to something that has not yet been mentioned, but is most important—the topic of your novel. It will not be arbitrary, even though that would certainly suit you best. I am sorry not to be able to give you a free hand here as I have in all other respects, but I am sure that it will not hamper you very much.

I cannot tell you what I expect you to write about immediately. You will only find out after you give your consent. Please do not think that any dishonorable intention lies behind this. You will see for yourself when the time comes that my reasons are not of a foul nature. Rest assured that the topic of the novel will be quite worthy of your masterly writing. In addition, it will be close to you and challenging.

I think that is all there is to say. Should you still have questions that require an answer, I am at your disposal. If not, I remain fervently hopeful that you will accept my proposal.

Sincerely,
Admirer

Any questions? The most important one was still unanswered. Why on earth would I agree to the ultimate authorial prostitution? What is this offer that cannot be refused? Why would I become a ghostwriter?

I had already started to type, but got no farther than "Esteemed Admi . . .". A sudden thought stopped me in the middle of the word, index finger hovering directly above the letter "r". My ears were filled with the thudding of my heart as I stared motionlessly at the monitor for a few moments, then erased the short text and closed the window. I put my elbows on the desk and began to rub my temples with my fingertips.

The topic of the commissioned novel! Of course! That was why he would only tell me after I consented. When it was too late to pull out. If he told me in advance, he would give himself away and my consent would not be forthcoming. He was completely aware of that. He had already tried to get it in another way, without success.

I still did not know who Admirer was, but he certainly was no stranger, rather someone I knew. Too well. More than was desired. That was the point.

It had to be one of the four: OpenSea, Banana, P-0 or Pandora. Someone who was more far-sighted than the others and had counted from the outset on the possibility that I might refuse to do what they were trying to get me to do. Someone who had devised a reserve plan and, just to be on the safe side, put it into play before the main one. Admirer had contacted me today before all the others.

Yes, but who? Who was hiding behind this mask? Who cared more than the others about getting what they wanted from me? Who was so arrogantly self-confident that they thought they could outwit me, that I would not find them out, that their game would succeed?

I knew where I should look for the answers to these questions: in Admirer's messages. I could not remember anything that aroused my suspicions. But I had read them with different eyes. Perhaps a new, more conscientious reading would turn something up.

I sent the cursor to the folder where I kept Admirer's emails, once again proud of my collector's mania. Without it, I would now be without a point of reference. I spent the next fifteen minutes carefully rereading the nine messages. Line by line. Between the lines. But in the end I was none the wiser.

I was clearly facing a serious adversary. He was very

careful about what he wrote. And how he wrote. I remembered what had first come to mind when I started
corresponding with Admirer. *Language is a telling indication about people.* Here the polished treatment was
not only a manner but a subterfuge as well. Hiding
behind it, the original voice could not be recognized.

The four original voices were kept in other folders. I
thought of rereading all of today's emails, but did not
have to waste my time. It was enough to concentrate on
the last message. If there was a trail anywhere, that was
the only place it could be.

I opened the four emails, marked passages that interested me, then copied them one under the other on
a blank page of the word processor. I wrote the author's
name under each of them. I did not care to save the file.
I crossed my arms and slowly started to read.

*If you're stubborn, though, there's a cure for that too.
(OpenSea)*.

*But you are terribly mistaken if you think my naïveté
is endless. Even though I was besotted, I had enough presence of mind to provide for myself should you leave me in
the lurch. You'll soon see how. You will acknowledge your
paternity whether you like it or not.*
(Banana)

*I will spare you from further insistence that we write
a book together, but I will not give up hope. Miracles do
happen. Indeed, not always by themselves. Sometimes they
need a little assistance . . .*
(P-0)

*Is there any other solution? Perhaps one, but it is not
honorable either. If only despair weren't compelling me to
take that route. Please forgive me . . .*
(Pandora)

All four had announced, in different tones, that they had an ace up their sleeve that they would now pull out after the failure of their attempts to get me to do what they wanted.

At first glance, Banana was the most suspicious. She had sent a clear warning. And her motives were the strongest. She had invested enormous effort in writing a novel that was missing a key part and evidently was unable to finish it. In addition, she had been spinning a web around me for quite some time. She had started even before we met. And finally, this double game matched her character the most.

OpenSea had threatened me too, although in a subtler way. Even though I could not rely on the impartiality of my intuition, I could not ignore its insistent whispering to suspect him above all. It reminded me that envy is no less powerful a motive than frustration at being unable to finish a novel. An envy that had been smoldering and gnawing inside for a long time. The only remedy for it was to denigrate the writing that was its cause. And what better way to do this than to get the author to demean himself—to parody his own work? One other thing set OpenSea apart. He above all would be able to compose Admirer's letters so skillfully that not a trace of his own self was left. Nothing strange. He among all of them was the only real writer, regardless of what I thought about his work.

Judging by the words on the screen in front of me, P-0 appeared the most reasonable. There was no trace of a threat. He just spoke vaguely about miracles that needed a little assistance. But that could easily be cunning. Someone would act like that if they wanted to remain inconspicuous. His motives, however, were certainly not negligible. He had bound himself so much to my writing that it was highly doubtful that he could write independently. Unless I agreed to that twisted partnership with him, he would be lost. Destined to lasting anonymity. In addition, he alone had mentioned "pay" and "price".

My intuition also had something to say about Pandora. It didn't whisper but shouted at the top of its lungs. It's not her! It's not her! The reason she was taken off the list of suspects was obvious. How could that poor old lady, the retired piano teacher, the very personification of innocence and honesty, even if a little twisted, devise and carry out wily and wicked plans? Particularly now, when her dog was on his deathbed! What nonsense! But it wasn't wise to rely on my intuition here either. It was blinded by its partiality for the old woman. Wasn't it Pandora who said that in her despair she was ready to forget honor? And is there any deeper despair than coming face to face with death? Even the most ordinary people are ready for anything when in its grips. Finally, there was one more reason why I did not dare neglect her. If this were a thriller, she would be suspicious for the very fact that she was the least suspicious.

So what was next? How could I figure out which of the four suspects was Admirer? They all had strong motives, they all had expressed their readiness to carry out their intention in some other way. At the same time, there were extenuating circumstances for each one. They were not all equally suspicious, but nothing pointed decisively at one of them. Or at least I had not noticed it.

Had my detective skills been better honed, I might have found my way through this uncertainty, noting a faint trace that led me forward. As things stood, the only idea that occurred to me as my next move was not particularly ingenious. What would happen, I wondered, if I sent each of them the same short email:

You are Admirer.

They would all deny it, of course, but the culprit would at least know I was on his heels. Taken aback at being discovered, he might give himself away somehow. It would probably be the one who used the most words to counter my claim. Then again, no. I underestimated Admirer. If he had been able to hide his identity in nine emails, it was unlikely that he would give himself away recklessly just because I had pointed a desperate finger at him.

It was quite possible that he would give the shortest reply. The replies from those who had been falsely accused would give me a headache too. The thought of the extensive explanations that would inevitably follow my enigmatic message was by no means pleasant. No, this would not be a good move.

And then I realized that I did not have to take a blind shot with three incidental victims. I could target Admirer himself. I had a line of fire that led right to him. I interlaced my fingers, cracked my knuckles and then started to type rapidly.

Esteemed Admirer,

What is that offer that cannot be refused?

Sincerely,
Writer

There was no reason to ramble and beat about the bush. We had reached the heart of the matter. Now we would see what was supposed to make me do the most shameful thing a writer could do. Betray the holiest of holies. Hand over the authorship of his own work. Sell his soul.

Admirer might not be tricking me. There really might be authors who agree to such things. It might truly be just a question of price. But even if that was so, I still had no clue as to what kind of proposal would make me turn my back on myself. I hoped I would not have to wait too long for the answer. Indeed, the gong resounded soon after.

Highly Esteemed Writer,

I told you that I did my homework. I know everything about you that is necessary for this arrangement. Even what you are convinced that no one knows. Your deepest secret.

The secret about the drought that has lasted too long.

You would give your eyeteeth for it to end, wouldn't you? To be carried once again by the strong, rapidly advancing floodwater.

The flood is my proposal.

One word from you is enough—and you will be inundated the very next moment.

Sincerely,
Admirer

My ears were drumming again as I vainly tried to put my jumbled thoughts in order. Crazy questions bombarded me from all around. They collided head on, fighting for priority. But before any single one prevailed, the drumming started to subside. Soon it was completely gone and a deep silence resounded. It was easy to recognize its distinctiveness.

My index finger trembled slightly as it headed towards the keys. Thank heavens it only had to type something brief.

Esteemed Admirer,
(I could have addressed him by another name now, but I would leave that for the end. I would otherwise have to open a new folder in my email archive.)

What would you like me to write about?

Sincerely,
Writer

The moment I clicked on the icon to send the message, calico fur rose above the edge of the desk. I was unable to prevent the chain collision of the cell phone, calculator and air conditioning remote control. As he stopped in front of the monitor, Felix turned towards me and gave me that look of his that immediately dispels any sign of anger.

We looked at each other up close for a few moments and then he brought his head near and rubbed his nose against me. I put out my hand just in time to hold him so he would not fall over the keyboard. That was his way of telling me that he was no longer angry, that he had forgiven me, that we loved each other again. I kissed him between his ears.

When he headed for the laptop the next moment, I had to act quickly. It was open and Felix could not lie on it right away. There was one more message to be sent from there. It was not easy to type because the tomcat thought I wanted to play and tried to catch my index finger as it flew over the small keyboard. Luckily, this email was not long either.

Highly Esteemed Writer,

About Felix, of course. Didn't I tell you that the topic would be close to you and challenging? And it will match the pseudonym.

Sincerely,
Admirer

After I had sent the message, I closed the laptop. Felix climbed onto his hard bed at once. Just like every day, he would sleep there for the next several hours. I stroked the left side of his mustache. He replied with a soft purring and then started to lick himself languidly. His noon wash never lasts long.

Before I got down to work, I had to send four more messages. Each one would bear good tidings. They would not have to force me to do anything.

I would tell OpenSea that I was starting to write a parody of my fiction. It would not really be that, but it could be understood that way. He is good at interpreting texts. Banana would be cheered by the fact that I was working on the pivotal chapter. It would not connect anything, but at least her son would not be fatherless. P-0 would be happy to learn that he would soon have a new book as a basis for a pastiche. He could even count on it being a pastiche of a pastiche of a pastiche. Why not? All for the advancement of literature. Finally, Pandora would be thrilled to hear of Felix's sudden change of heart. Not only had he unexpectedly started to love my writing, but he was thrilled that he, along with Albert, was to be the hero of my new novel.

The gong brought me out of my thoughts. I was just about to reach for the mouse and open my virtual mailbox, but the movement was left unfinished. There was no need to check who had sent the message. I also did not have to hurry and save it. It was not going anywhere.

Instead, my hand continued towards the middle speaker and turned it off. The email alert would only interfere with my writing. It was time to come to my senses.

Contributors

About the author

Zoran Živković was born in Belgrade, Serbia, on October 5, 1948. Until his recent retirement, he was a full professor at the Faculty of Philology, the University of Belgrade, teaching creative writing. He is one of the most translated contemporary Serbian writers: by the end of 2019 there were more than 100 foreign editions of his books of fiction, published in 23 countries, in 20 languages.

Živković has won several literary awards for his fiction, beginning with the Miloš Crnjanski award in 1994 for his novel *The Fourth Circle*. In 2003, Živković's mosaic novel *The Library* won a World Fantasy Award for Best Novella; in 2007 his novel *The Bridge* won the Isidora Sekulić award; and in 2007 he received the Stefan Mitrov Ljubiša award for lifetime achievement in literature. In 2014 and 2015 he received three awards for his contribution to the literature of fantastika: Art-Anima, Stanislav Lem and The Golden Dragon.

Zoran Živković has been recognized with his selection as European Grand Master for 2017 by the European Science Fiction Society at the 39th Eurocon in Dortmund, Germany.

Živković is the author of the 22 books of fiction:
  The Fourth Circle (1993)
  Time Gifts (1997)
  The Writer (1998)
  The Book (1999)
  Impossible Encounters (2000)
  Seven Touches of Music (2001)
  The Library (2002)
  Steps through the Mist (2003)
  Hidden Camera (2003)
  Compartments (2004)
  Four Stories till the End (2004)
  Twelve Collections and the Teashop (2005)
  The Bridge (2006)
  Miss Tamara, The Reader (2006),
  Amarcord (2007)
  The Last Book (2007)
  Escher's Loops (2008)
  The Ghostwriter (2009)
  The Five Wonders of the Danube (2011)
  The Grand Manuscript (2012)
  The Compendium of the Dead (2015)
  The Image Interpreter (2016)

About the artist

Youchan Ito was born 1968 in Aichi prefecture, Japan. She launched her career as a graphic designer in 1988, becoming a freelancer illustrator in 1991 and founding Togoru Co., Ltd. with her husband in 2000. In 2017 the company was reborn as Togoru Art Works. She works with a wide range of genres including cover art and design for science fiction, mysteries and horror titles, as well as illustrations for children's books.

www.youchan.com